THE EARL'S TEMPTING WARD

Dukes Gone Dirty
Book 2

Bella Moxie

ARE YOU SIGNED UP FOR DRAGONBLADE'S BLOG?

You'll get the latest news and information on exclusive giveaways, exclusive excerpts, coming releases, sales, free books, cover reveals and more.

Check out our complete list of authors, too!

No spam, no junk. That's a promise!

Sign Up Here

www.dragonbladepublishing.com

Dearest Reader;

Thank you for your support of a small press. At Dragonblade Publishing, we strive to bring you the highest quality Historical Romance from some of the best authors in the business. Without your support, there is no 'us', so we sincerely hope you adore these stories and find some new favorite authors along the way.

Happy Reading!

CEO, Dragonblade Publishing

Additional Dragonblade books by Author Bella Moxie

Dukes Gone Dirty Series
The Duke's Defiant Angel (Book 1)
The Earl's Tempting Ward (Book 2)

CHAPTER ONE

*B*ANG!

Benedict winced as sounds of the ruined wing's reconstruction reached his study.

He could not say for sure which of his ancestors who'd preceded him as the Earl of Foster had been so very fond of gothic architecture, but he cursed that fellow now.

It was impossible to find a moment's peace in this drafty old manor.

Head bent over the stack of legal documents before him, he tried to ignore the workers' voices that echoed off the vaulted ceilings outside his study door. His mother's voice stood out in stark contrast. High and sharp, her commands were staccato chirps amidst the low, booming bass tones of the workers she was ordering about.

Doing what, exactly?

He pinched the bridge of his nose with a sigh. He should probably find out.

Not that his input was required. He and his mother had come to a sort of silent truce these past weeks since he'd returned from his failed trip to London. She left him in peace, and he stayed out of her way as she went about her business.

Her business seemed to be the Sisyphean task of keeping this old manor up to snuff with all the current trends and new-fashioned trappings.

Staying out of one another's way had been working well for them—far better than the taut silences and tense conversations they'd suffered through for months after the tragedy.

It had been those encounters, fraught with unspoken accusations and riddled with guilt, that had driven him to London in the first place. Well, that and his friends' persistence. His former schoolmates had harassed him into joining them in town to seek out a wife.

His friend the Duke of Raffian had declared this the season that their band of rogues finally leave behind their carousing to assume the mantle and sire some heirs.

It shouldn't have been difficult—indeed, Raff had not only found himself a bride, he'd gone and fallen in love with the girl. But even with the title of earl attached to his person, Benedict hadn't been able to shake the whispers and the stares. It was enough to drive a man mad.

Or back to his family estate, at least.

The sound of heavy footsteps on the marble floors carried to him so clearly, it was as if he were attempting to peruse these documents right smack in the midst of the entrance hall.

What were they doing out there?

Something clattered. A shout carried.

Benedict fell back in his seat with a sigh. Perhaps he ought to have stayed in London.

But no. He dismissed the thought as quickly as it arrived. The townhouse in Mayfair might have been quieter, with its thick oriental rugs, small rooms, and heavy curtains, but that hardly made up for the stares.

Out of habit, he ran a hand over the uneven and unnaturally smooth skin of his left jaw.

No, he did not wish to be back there where the hushed whispers of the *ton* were far louder than these echoes and shouts could ever be.

Eventually, mercifully, the sounds grew distant. The workers were heading upstairs, thank God. He narrowed his eyes and focused on the words before him with renewed focus. For approximately two seconds. That was how much of a reprieve he was allotted before a sharp knock on his study door interrupted him.

Before he could reply, the door was thrown open. His mother stood there, dark and dour, and for a moment, he was shocked at the sight of her. Not only because she'd been keeping her distance this past week, not setting foot in this room which had once been his father's private domain, but also because he still wasn't quite used to the change in her appearance.

The fire that had claimed his father and older brother's lives hadn't left her with the sort of visible scars that he carried, but it had changed her just as drastically. Overnight, it seemed, she'd gone from a vibrant lady and proud matron to...well, *this*.

A pale imitation of her former self. A sad one. A bitter one. One filled with hatred...for him.

"Mother," he said evenly, quickly hiding his surprise at her sudden appearance.

She pinched her lips as if the word "Mother" were an insult.

A muscle worked in his jaw as a familiar heavy tension settled between them.

She'd never been the sort one would call cheerful. The lady was a countess, after all, and she'd embodied that. She'd been gracious, if not warm, with a steady disposition not prone to extreme emotions one way or the other.

But now as the dowager countess, she seemed a hollow version of her former charismatic self. Gray strands had begun to cobweb their way through her ink-black hair, aging her overnight, and deep creases now marred sharp features so like his own.

She'd been attractive once.

But then again, so had he.

Now she bore remnants of grief. A constant reminder that her life had been devastated. By him. Her youngest son. The one who was meant to be the spare.

The tight skin around his scars itched as if reminding him of their presence. As if he could ever forget.

She regarded him with a sour expression from where she still hesitated in the doorway, and that was it, he realized. This hesitation was what was so different about her now, even more than the physical signs of aging.

His mother had never been one to hesitate before. Certainly not around him. She might not have been an affectionate mother, but she'd been comfortable with both Benedict and his brother, Robert.

More so with Robert, but that was to be expected. He'd been the eldest, and the heir—not to mention the dutiful, obedient son.

And now the dead son.

She seemed to overcome whatever it was that had been holding her prisoner in the doorway, and he waited with quiet unease for her to speak.

"You've been in here all morning," she said.

It came out as an accusation.

"So I have," he agreed.

Her gaze drifted away from his as if against her will. Her lips rolled inward, her mouth pinching at the edges. This room had been her husband's solace. His domain. The room where he'd spent most of his days and where he'd gone about his business.

Benedict hadn't seen his mother enter this room once since the accident.

"Did you need something, Mother?"

Her gaze snapped back to his, and he saw it. Before she could hide her anger, he saw it. Truthfully, it was always there just under the surface. The blame. The anger.

She straightened, her chin coming up in a stubborn set. "Will you be joining us for dinner this evening?"

He frowned. *Us?*

This was the first time in many months that his mother had made any attempt to dine with him. A fact that might have been oozed venom, and her eyes flashed with anger.

Silence fell between them, the sort of silence that had been eating him alive for nearly a year. Surely London hadn't been worse than this. Had it?

He took a deep breath and met her withering glare. There was a challenge in her eyes. One she didn't think he'd be able to meet.

He leaned forward, anger flaring up beneath the guilt and the shame. "Fine," he snapped. "So now I have a spoiled little brat on my hands. Wonderful." He rose from his seat. "Know this. I will not tolerate tantrums or misbehaving, is that clear?"

She arched a brow, unimpressed. "And you think you are one to discipline her?"

The derisive mockery in her gaze stung. She didn't think him fit to keep a single child in line let alone manage an earldom.

"If this Philippa so much as speaks out of turn, I will do as I must," he said. "Orphan child or not, I will take that girl over my knee."

"Oh dear." A soft voice filled the air, and a stunning young lady with dark red hair and sparkling green eyes stepped into the doorway just behind his mother. Her gaze landed on him, as long lashes batted against high cheekbones and lush red lips curved up in a smile that somehow managed to be both sweet and wicked.

His mother gasped with surprise at her sudden arrival, but Benedict stood silent, speechless in the face of the beauty before him.

"You must be Lord Foster," she said with the slightest twinge of an accent. Her voice wrapped around him, low and smooth like velvet.

Heat speared through him like a knife, the shock of it sudden and savage. Her eyes glinted with mischief, and her lips curled up at the corners at his shocked silence.

Wicked. Definitely wicked.

"I am Miss Philippa Lorezon…" She took a step forward, her eyes narrowing slightly on him. "And I promise I'll do my very best to behave." Her lips parted, and her eyes widened in exaggerated innocence. "I certainly wouldn't wish for you to have to spank me, my lord."

CHAPTER TWO

T HE GREAT AND powerful earl she'd heard so much about glared at her from behind his desk, and Philippa could not blame him. It was such a naughty thing to say.

But then again, she *was* rather wicked, a fact she'd learned to embrace after fighting it for so very long. Still, heat filled her cheeks as she heard her parents' chastisements ringing in the back of her mind, shaming her more thoroughly than this large beast of an earl could ever hope to do.

Not that Lord Foster's glower wasn't formidable. It was. And his broad shoulders and large build were terribly intimidating. Scars marred the left side of his face, making what must have been a handsome face something warped and terrifying.

He must have been striking before the accident. That much was clear. Sharp nose, high cheekbones, a heavy brow. Striking and formidable. But add in the scars and that fiery glare, and it was no wonder the workers had stared at her in wide-eyed horror when she'd informed them that she'd find the master of the house herself.

Hadn't been difficult to do. Just follow the growl. She'd half expected to find a feral animal in this study. Instead, she'd found *him*. The Earl of Foster. Threatening to take her over his knee.

A surge of heat coiled low in her belly as a lewd image formed in her mind. She bit her lip and felt his gaze drop to her lips to follow the movement.

"My dear, you gave us a start," the dowager countess said.

Philippa dipped into a curtsy, head down as she murmured a greeting and an apology for having surprised them.

The earl still hadn't yet spoken. He hadn't moved from behind the desk either. He just stood there and glared at her as though she were a rodent infesting this monstrous castle of theirs.

"You'll have to forgive my son the inhospitable welcome," Lady Foster said. "He was not aware of your arrival today, and I'm afraid he did not inherit his father's charm nor his grace."

"Not at all, my lady," she said, her gaze flicking over to see how this large brute of a man took to being insulted by his mother in front of a stranger.

He didn't appear to have heard. His expression hadn't altered; his glare still burned into her skin.

Had she shocked him with her comment? She supposed most ladies would have ignored the comment they'd overheard. Feigned deafness if need be. That was her mother's favorite trick whenever anyone said anything untoward.

What was that? Oh, my apologies, I could not hear you.

That was how she'd avoided dealing with anything unpleasant. She'd feigned ignorance in company and went both deaf and blind when it came to her own daughter. Easier to pretend Philippa didn't exist than to face the fact that she'd sired a wayward, immoral creature.

And she was. She'd learned the hard way that it was useless to deny her wicked nature.

She'd long known that her father had been right when he'd call her their little devil. It was the red hair, her father had claimed.

He'd been superstitious like that.

The dowager countess was remarking on the suddenness of her arrival, asking after her journey.

Lord Foster continued to stare.

She smiled sweetly as she waited for the earl to recover from the shock. He'd berate her, no doubt, for having sought him out rather than waiting meekly in the entrance hall. For having dared to utter the words "spank me" in his esteemed company.

A horrible urge to laugh stole over her, but it fled just as quickly, replaced once more by the dark heavy weight that had been hanging over her ever since her parents' death one year before.

The year of mourning was over, and this was it. This was her life now.

Stuck with the man her mother had referred to as "that dreadful Lord Benedict" when she was being kind. She'd relate the contents of her dear friend's correspondence with a sad shake of her head. *Such a shame poor Lady Foster sired such an incorrigible rogue. Seems he's nothing at all like his elder brother.*

Oh yes, Philippa had heard all the stories from her mother about that dreadful younger son.

Rake, reprobate, and *wastrel* were all terms she'd come to associate with the man before her. And that was *before* the notorious fire which had taken his already wretched reputation and made it outright infamous. She might have been in mourning this past year, but even she had heard tales of the nefarious younger brother who'd inherited a title and its fortune after a mysterious tragedy.

No one had outright said that he was to blame, as far as she knew…but it was clearly suspected.

His eyes seemed to darken as if he could read her thoughts. Oh my, but he did have a fearsome visage. It wouldn't stretch the imagination to think him capable of murder.

And this was the man who was meant to look after her. How very fitting.

Philippa waited patiently for him to finish his perusal. His lips curled up in a sneer, and dark, cold eyes raked over her.

All those dreams she'd had for her future. And instead, she was here.

The little devil had been sent to hell.

For the best. Well deserved, really. She squared her shoulders. Might as well make herself comfortable.

"Mother," he growled, his gaze never leaving Philippa. "You did not tell me she was grown."

Philippa pressed her lips together to hold back a smile. He sounded so very put off by the fact. As if being *grown* was a sin.

"Well," his mother fussed. "I didn't say she was a child either."

"You most certainly did."

His harsh tone as he turned to face his mother had Philippa flinching. Not in fear. She wasn't afraid of anyone. Not anymore. The only good thing to come of losing everything and everyone she loved? There was nothing left to lose, which meant nothing to fear.

But she recoiled at the way this overbearing brute was speaking to his mother, as if she were his servant or his enemy, even.

"You called her a child," he said, his voice a menacing threat. *"Poor babe,* I believe you said."

His tone was mocking, but the dowager countess held her head high. "I am old, Benedict. To me, *you* are a child."

A silence fell that had Philippa twitching with discomfort. She had the disturbing suspicion that a conversation was taking place in that silence between them, and it was not a pleasant tête-à-tête.

Eventually, he looked away from his mother, and when his gaze fell on Philippa again, she felt it burn through the thick wool of her traveling gown. That glare was judgment itself, and she'd come out wanting.

"What am I to do with a grown woman?" he snapped.

I have some ideas. Philippa swallowed down the words before they could escape. *Naughty, naughty Philippa.*

She'd thought she'd learned her lesson, but it seemed there was some part of her too wicked to learn, even now. Even after everything she'd done.

After everything she'd ruined.

"You'll take her to London, of course," the dowager countess said.

The look of horror on Lord Foster's face might have been humorous…if it wasn't so terribly foreboding.

He *would* take her to London, wouldn't he? He did not expect her to languish here in this miserable, empty house forever…did he?

His gaze found hers as if he could hear her thoughts.

Perhaps he did.

She swallowed thickly. Maybe he thought to hold her prisoner here. To have her do his bidding and be his indentured servant.

Her mind—that unceasingly wicked mind—it chose that moment to call up every scandalous book she'd stolen from Herr Heinrich's collection. A friend of her father's, his terribly hidden secret library had been eye-opening, to say the least. Her mother likely wished Philippa had stayed behind on that last tour of the continent.

Far too many libraries for her to pillage.

But then again, the real damage to her heart and her soul had taken place in Italy, in the safety of her own home.

She wondered what her parents would think of that ironic twist.

They'd think nothing because they are dead.

She nearly tsked aloud at her own wayward thoughts. Her mother was the religious one, her father, the superstitious sort. She was neither. All she believed in was what she saw around her. Cause and effect. Actions and repercussions.

Mistakes and consequences.

That's what this was.

She let her gaze wander around the room. Let this giant beast glare. Let the countess speak of her as if she were not there. It hardly mattered in the end. She would not be here long—as Lady Foster was so succinctly pointing out.

"She needs to find a husband," the dowager countess was saying in a hushed voice as if perhaps Philippa could not hear. Or maybe the servants were not to know that she was a pathetic and lonely orphan in need of a protector?

"And?" The man she was beginning to think of as Lord Arse shot back.

"And you must take her."

He stared at her for so long, Philippa fidgeted on the older woman's behalf.

"You can be her chaperone," he said. His gaze flickered over to Philippa, a hint of wariness there like he was waiting for her to swoon or weep or something of the sort.

Perhaps he thought she'd be offended by his rude welcome. Indeed, she was not. It was rather a relief to have such a crass, unfeeling gentleman as her guardian. Ever since her parents' death, she'd been surrounded by sympathy and kindness. So much kindness she thought she might drown in it.

His lack of civility, even the harshness of his countenance and the cruelty in his glare—it fell over her like a gust of fresh air.

She wanted more of it.

That part of her that was always needy, always seeking more…it sat up at attention now.

Down, girl.

The dowager countess was still hissing at her son under her breath. "I am in mourning."

"And I am not?" he snapped.

The whip of his voice had Philippa returning to the conversation with a jolt.

His mother barely even noticed, continuing as if he hadn't interrupted.

So, this was his normal behavior then?

Wonderful.

"I will accompany you to London if you wish," the dowager countess was saying. "But we both know you need to return if you plan to find yourself a wife."

His jaw twitched slightly, and he cast Philippa a sidelong look.

She swallowed hard. So, he was in search of a wife then.

Interesting. She almost pitied the woman who'd be stuck with this gruff, growling beast.

Almost.

She could think of worse fates than being ensnared by that glare. She'd already decided that his coarseness was better than sweet sympathy.

Would he truly take a hand to her if she were to misbehave?

She nibbled on her lip, a heat pooling low in her belly.

He might.

And she found she wanted to test this threat. To push him to the breaking point and see just how cruel the dreadful lord could be.

His mother was still talking. About London. About his obligations. About what they owed her—or rather, her mother.

She didn't pay attention. Truthfully, she didn't much care. She would go where they told her. She would marry whomever they deemed fit.

She'd lost the right to protest, and she well knew it. It was her own fault she was here. Her own fault her parents were gone.

Apparently losing patience with his mother's speech about his obligations and responsibilities, the earl turned to look at the clock over the mantel, and in doing so, Philippa found herself staring head-on at the scarred, mutilated side of his face.

Her breath caught at the brutality of it. The rawness and the pain that could not be hidden.

Her stomach twisted—not with disgust but empathy.

The scars on his face were a physical, undeniable sign of his pain, and she was almost positive that she had the very same scars. But hers were hidden. Hers were deep inside where there was no light. Where there was only dark. Her wounds festered in that darkness. And as she stared at the earl's visible pain, she could have sworn she felt her own scars shriek in agony.

A sharp inhale escaped. Loud enough to draw his attention, and she did not look away quickly enough.

He caught her stare. And whatever he saw in her expression

and in her eyes, it had him sneering in her direction. The glare in his eyes wasn't just anger—it was hatred. Toward her.

She found herself backing away a step out of instinct.

She wasn't scared. But that didn't stop her body from responding to the sight of a predator in her midst.

A predator who looked as though he meant to rip her apart.

She tilted her head up. She had a feeling neither of them heard a word his mother was saying.

Didn't matter anyway. She'd go to London. She'd do whatever her guardian wished.

When he dismissed them both, she let the dowager countess lead her to her new room where her trunks were already waiting.

No one seemed to care if she spoke, so she kept quiet until the dowager countess informed her she would see her that night at dinner.

And then she left, and Philippa was once more alone.

The loneliness was the worst part of this new life she'd found herself in.

The loneliness was what threatened to crush her.

But she pushed all that aside and focused on examining the fusty old antiques that adorned this stale room. She'd seen the workers coming and going from the other wing—the one that had burned down.

She'd been told by the local woman who'd been sent to fetch her from the carriage that it was being rebuilt and would have all the modern trappings.

But for now, she was stuck here. In an ancient, seemingly forgotten room in an old, forbidding, mournful manor.

This was her hell.

Perfect.

Her hands trembled as she put her clothes away, dismissing the maid.

This was precisely where she belonged.

CHAPTER THREE

B ENEDICT HAD BEEN spending far too much time in the stables. Particularly when one considered he did not have much of an interest in horseflesh. Not a keen fascination, at any rate.

And he certainly had never had any desire to witness a foaling.

"Bloody hell," he muttered as the stable boy beside him looked on with wide eyes.

The large mare couldn't be stopped, this much he knew. Nature was at work. He grimaced as he watched the mare snort, plumes of steam leaving her nostrils in the cold, late-March air.

"Where's your master, boy?" he asked the child.

Dark eyes gazed up at him blankly.

Was the boy a simpleton or merely too overwhelmed at being spoken to by an earl? Benedict turned away with a sigh. Perhaps neither. The lad was no doubt terrified of the scarred beast who stood before him—the evil man who'd ruined the manor and killed his own family.

Good God, he'd actually done it. He'd become the monster children were warned about. He *was* the cautionary bedtime tale.

The thought had him huffing with wry amusement. "Go on," he said to the boy. "Go find a groom or the stablemaster."

The child did not need to be told twice. He fled as if the devil was on his heels.

Benedict looked around him. Where was everyone?

Likely avoiding him. He crossed his arms and glared at the mare, willing the beast to halt immediately. He'd not come out here to witness the miracle of birth, for God's sake. He'd just been…

Hiding.

Blast it all. What was the use in denying it? He'd been avoiding his new ward all week, and more often than not, that drove him out of the house. As it was still cold outside, he'd taken to visiting the stables.

Surely, she wouldn't follow him here.

Not that Philippa was *following* him, necessarily. It was just that with half the manor under construction and the weather so dark and dreary this past week, it was difficult to avoid one another.

His mother, however, managed to keep her distance as usual. While she was off doing what she deemed to be her dowager countess duty, he'd been caught in an odd and awkward sort of dance trying to steer clear of the young lady in his care.

He winced as the mare pawed at the ground. "Please wait," he said quietly. "I implore you."

"Wait for what?" Philippa's voice behind him had him turning with a start.

She greeted him with a smile that was all sunshine and innocence.

That smile made his gut twist with wariness.

"What are you doing here?" he asked.

Christ, he hadn't meant to sound so rude. He looked from her to the mare and back again. "This is no place for a gently bred young lady."

Her smile grew, her green eyes sparkling in a way that had come to make his muscles tense as if for a blow.

She was innocent, and she was sheltered. But there was something in her, beneath the surface, that hinted at danger.

Her gait was slow and her demeanor not at all alarmed by the sight of the pacing mare before her as she moved further into the stables. "What if that gently bred young lady was raised in the country and spent an inordinate amount of time in the stables?"

His brows hitched. "Did you?"

Her small smile was smug. There was a hint of the feline about her with her high, sharp cheekbones and her narrow nose, and the way her eyes were slightly narrowed and upturned at the edges. And then there were her eyes themselves. Her eyes fairly gleamed like a cat's when caught in a lantern's glow.

"The way I see it, I was destined to spend time in the stables," she said with a little smile that made him feel like they were talking about something—anything, really—other than horses and stables.

"Er, pardon?" he said, his voice little more than a growl. But damn it all to hell she looked pretty in the cold. Her cheeks were flushed the same pink as her lips, and little wisps of auburn and red hair danced around her like a halo.

"The name," she said, stripping her gloves off as she slowly approached the anxious mare. "Philippa means lover of horses." Her tone was distracted as she reached out to calm the horse. "I used to tell my father it was his own fault for bequeathing me such a name." There was a hint of laughter in her voice, but he saw the sadness in her smile.

He'd gone out of his way to avoid her this week, it was true. But in those rare occasions when he couldn't avoid her—at meals, mostly, when his mother was present, if mostly silent.

All three of them were silent, for the most part.

Even so, she'd never spoken of her parents. Though, as she was just now coming out of mourning, he supposed that was to be expected. He and his mother rarely spoke of their deceased family either. What was there to say?

Her gaze turned to meet his, and he felt her scrutiny like a blow to the gut.

"Would you like my assistance?" she asked.

It was a polite question, but the small smile that hovered over her lips made his thoughts go someplace dark and dirty. As if she were offering to help him find pleasure. As if she were offering something that had nothing to do with horses and foaling.

He turned to glower at the open door where the stable boy had fled. Bloody hell, he shouldn't be in here alone with her.

His mind was addled, surely.

When he glanced back at her, there were nothing but innocent, helpful questions in her eyes. She was seeking permission, nothing more.

So why was it that when she was near, his entire body felt like it had been struck by lightning? Why did her smiles and her glances and the soft sway of her hips make him feel like he was being seduced?

It was lunacy.

But when her lips curved up and her eyes met his…lunacy or not, he ached for her.

He'd be attracted to this woman no matter what. She had a figure that made his hands itch to grab her hips, bend her over, and fuck her senseless, and no one could deny her beauty. But it was that whiff of danger, the wicked gleam in her eyes—there and gone in a heartbeat—and the way she seemed to crackle with seductive energy.

It was that which had him avoiding her. It was that air of mischief and curiosity that made him doubt his own willpower around her. It had been too long since he'd been with a woman. Not since the night of the fire. All it would take was one lingering touch, one poor decision…

Hell. All she had to do was smile sweetly at him right now, and his manhood strained, begging for her touch.

She tilted her head to the side and studied him as he studied her. "Perhaps I can help."

Blast. For a moment he'd forgotten entirely about the mare.

"I don't believe that will be necessary," he said. "The stablemaster shall be along shortly, and while I don't know much about these things, there's still some time before—"

He was interrupted by the sound of a large amount of liquid hitting the dirt floor.

"Bloody hell!" He leapt back a foot as the mare came down to the ground.

To his surprise, Philippa laughed.

He turned toward her at the low, husky sound. He stared at her for a long moment, taking in the curve of her lips, the glint of laughter in her eyes.

Laughter at *his* expense.

He frowned, and her laughter quieted.

"You were saying?" she teased.

He turned his attention to the horse, though the beast definitely did not care that he was glaring.

"It won't be long now," Philippa said, coming to kneel by the horse's head, lowering her voice and seemingly not noticing at all that she was squatting in the dirt.

Benedict cast a helpless glance around for any sign of the stablemaster. Hell, he'd take that dimwitted stable boy at this point.

"No more than twenty minutes, I'd say." Philippa glanced up at him with another smile. Like this was good news.

She was smiling expectantly, but he had nothing to say to this, so he gave a grunt of acknowledgment.

Inexplicably, she grinned even wider as if he'd just said something clever.

Philippa turned back to the mare, and a moment later, the gray-haired, old stablemaster was hurrying into the stables and shooing them both away. "Oh no, no, my lady," he was mumbling as he helped Philippa to her feet. "This is no place for a lady."

He didn't say the same to Benedict—likely because the man valued his job—but Benedict wasn't at all put out to be leaving the mare and its forthcoming foal behind.

"Come along, Philippa," he said, ignoring her weary sigh as she trailed behind him.

"I do not see why I could not stay."

He cast her a sidelong glance, torn between amusement and irritation at her petulant tone. "Because it is not fit for a lady, as the stablemaster said."

"Mmm," she said, walking so close her sleeve brushed his. "And when it is my time to have a child? Will I be allowed in the room, do you suppose? Or will it be too much for my delicate nerves?"

He stopped walking, staring at her in shock.

Her head fell back with a laugh. "I've scandalized you, haven't I?"

He snapped his jaw shut, glowering down at her. "I was told you were a lady, Miss Lo—"

"Oh, it's Philippa, please," she said, her tone beseeching.

He glared down at her. Not because he was so very outraged but because he was puzzled by the riddle before him.

So sweet and innocent one moment and then delighting in shocking him the next.

Her gaze turned knowing as she peeked up at him coyly from beneath her lashes. "Have I misbehaved?"

Her voice was breathy and low. The voice of a woman in bed. His gut tightened with a hot wave of lust as he pictured it. Her red hair spread around her on a pillow. Those green eyes shuttered by half-lowered lids. Her lips parted and her legs spread wide and—

Bloody hell. He turned away abruptly. Yes, it had definitely been far too long since he'd taken a woman, and this little chit was too tempting by far.

And the worst part was, he was beginning to suspect she knew it.

Her lips taunted him as she pouted. "I have been naughty, haven't I?" She sidled closer.

He ought to back away but he couldn't. His erection was stiff and painful, and the scent of her held him captive.

"Are you very angry with me?" she said in that breathy whisper. She rested a hand on his arm and let her head fall back, revealing the creamy length of her neck. "Will you be forced to take me over your knee?"

Christ. He jerked away then, but it was too late. His mind was filled with the image. Her skirts tossed up, her undergarments discarded. Her ripe little ass wriggling in his lap as he gave her a spanking.

His throat was too dry to swallow, and his gaze had fallen to her lips.

They parted, and then he caught the tip of her pink tongue darting out to wet her lips.

When he finally tore his gaze away to look into her eyes, he was stunned speechless. Her eyes were wide with wonder and...fear?

Of course she was afraid. He did not need a looking glass to know how repulsive he was, particularly this close and looming over her as he was.

With a muttered curse he took a step back.

She was laughing at him.

Again.

His lungs hitched. This time was different though. This time she was taunting him, he was sure of it. Laughing at him for desiring her when he was so hideous himself.

For a moment, he couldn't tear his gaze away; he was so mystified by the slight little thing. She was as changeable as the wind. So many personalities in one.

Which was she? Sheltered innocent or seductive little harlot?

In the end, did it matter? Either way, she was his ward. His responsibility.

Even if she were a woman of experience. Even if she actually desired him in return—unlikely as that might be. It wouldn't change the fact that she was his to protect, not his to touch.

"Come along," he commanded, his voice too gruff and curt as he turned away.

"Oh, but my lord..." Her tone was wheedling, but when her

hand came to his arm again, he stopped to glare at her.

"I don't know what you're playing at, little girl, but this game of yours stops now," he said.

Her eyes widened, and she blinked in the face of his anger. "I haven't done anything—"

"Bullocks."

Her lips pinched together at the oath.

He leaned down closer, even though he knew he was tempting his own willpower by being this close to those luscious lips. "You think to mock me with a flirtation, is that it?"

Her brows arched, and he caught honest confusion in her eyes. "N-no, I didn't—"

She stopped when he grabbed her hand, bare now after she'd taken off her gloves to stroke the mare's flesh. Her lips parted in surprise, and he just barely bit back a groan.

Those lips. Lord, but he ached to taste them. He'd bury his hands in that thick hair and claim them with his own and—

He looked away with a sharp hiss. The moment they arrived in London, he'd find a whore, that's what he'd do. Not a mistress—no decent woman in her right mind would want his scarred body on top of hers. But a cheap whore down on Vestry Lane. One who'd go on her knees and take him into her mouth until he purged all thoughts of his tempting little ward.

Philippa tugged on her hand, and only then did he realize he still held it.

A bitter, twisted urge rose up in him. He didn't want to see her mockery, but he had a perverse desire to see her disgust. He lifted her hand to touch his scars, savoring a sick satisfaction when she gasped.

Horror. That was what she felt when she looked at him.

"Still want me to take you over my knee, little girl?" This time he was the one taunting, and he didn't try to hide it. Just like he didn't make any attempt to hide the wicked desire that had his manhood straining toward her like she was its master.

"I-I—"

He leaned down closer, so close he could feel the heat of her breath. "Do you want to play with the devil, is that it, Philippa? Do you want to see how far you can go before you get burnt?"

"I didn't mean to…" She stopped to swallow and stumbled back a step when he released her hand. "I'm sorry."

Said in a whisper so soft and sweet, his anger and that sick satisfaction faded in a heartbeat leaving him cold.

He turned away.

"You're of an age to know better," he said as he headed toward the house. "Save your curiosity for your husband."

Your husband. The words made his lips curl into a sneer and a surge of anger he couldn't explain boil his blood.

"We leave in the morning," he said. "You'll need your rest." He paused to glance over his shoulder, taking in the sight of her, so fresh and pure and lovely. An angel in his midst.

Well, an angel with a wicked streak.

He hardened his expression, adopting his fiercest glare. "Go to your room."

CHAPTER FOUR

"**G**O TO YOUR room," Philippa muttered as she paced. "Go to your *room*?"

She hadn't gone to her room. Instead, she'd sought solace in the library, but solitude was not helping. With each new length she strode, she worked herself into a fine rage.

And the worst part was, there was no one on whom to lash out.

He'd just walked away.

She growled low in her throat as her footsteps echoed throughout the room.

She was glad they'd leave for London in the morning. This house would be the death of her with its empty halls and closed-off wings. She'd been living in grief for nearly a year now, but only on the inside. This manor, however, was filled with it. Grief was seeping from the ceilings and dripping down the walls.

She could barely breathe here. There was no escape from it. Except…

Except for those rare moments when the Earl of Foster deigned to speak to her. When he drove all the memories and the regrets far from her mind with a simple look. Or rather, a glare.

She stopped short in the middle of the room as her mind filled with the image of that glare. It would have been a ferocious glower even without the scars. But with them…

She shivered as a draft cut through the window beside her.

With them, he was outright fearsome.

But she wasn't afraid of him. Or…she hadn't been until his unflappably stern facade had dropped, and he'd made her touch his scars.

She rubbed her fingers together now, remembering the shocking feel of that smooth, rippled texture that was in such contrast to the rough stubble that had rubbed the sensitive skin of her inner wrist.

Rough and smooth. Hot and cold. Terrifying and gentle.

And yes, she had seen him be gentle. He'd kept his distance from the mare, but when she'd entered the stable, she'd seen it. A softening of his features. Worry. Concern.

Over a *horse*.

Granted, this was not much to go on. She wasn't about to nominate the man for sainthood. But it had tugged at her heart all the same.

It had her wondering, too. What would it be like if those coal-dark eyes were to soften with tenderness? What if that heat of desire were tempered with the warmth of affection?

A door closed in the hallway, and she spun around quickly at the sound, straining her ears to hear more.

When she didn't, she strode out into the hallway. The sound had come from his study.

Lord Foster was in there. And she'd long since lost any sense of reason. Anger had her marching to the closed door, knocking once before letting herself in.

He glanced up without so much as a flicker of surprise. "I thought I told you to go to your room."

"I am not a child." She made the massive mistake of ending this loud declaration with a stomp of her foot.

His irritatingly bland gaze traveled down the length of her skirts and landed at her feet. "Aren't you?"

Blast. He was so dreadfully knowing. And she'd never felt more helpless.

No. That wasn't true. She'd felt nothing *but* helpless since the accident. But this was different. She'd gotten a taste earlier…a taste of something delicious.

Every time she saw desire in his eyes, she tasted it anew. An escape. A distraction. A wave of sensations overwhelming enough to drown out everything else.

And for a little while there, she'd even had a taste of power. A feeling of control—raw and unwieldy—but control, nonetheless.

She'd seen the way he'd looked at her.

She'd seen the way he'd wanted her.

A thrill raced down her spine at the memory. She wanted to see it again. She wanted to see…anything, really. His anger, his desire, his rage. She'd take any emotion over this closed-off wall he'd erected to shut her out.

Not *just* her, she knew that. He treated his mother and the servants with the same apathetic, taciturn derision. As if none of them were of the same caliber as him. As if he alone knew pain and isolation.

She frowned at the thought. He had no idea. The arrogant fool had no notion of what anyone else was going through.

"Well?" He glanced up as if confused to find her still standing there. "Why not be a good girl and do as you're told?"

"Because I'm not a good girl," she said. She hated how childish she sounded, but he brought it out in her by treating her like a child. "I'm a grown woman. I'll be married soon enough—"

"Yes, and at that point, you'll be some other man's problem," he interjected smoothly. "But until then, you will do as I say."

Her hands twitched at her sides, and she fought the urge to form fists. But even as he annoyed her, her heart was pounding hard and fast.

This was what she'd come here for.

A reaction. A feeling. Something other than the bottomless pit of darkness that was forever threatening to drown her.

But it wasn't enough. She wanted a response from him, as well. She needed to see him lose his control. Anger, passion, joy, it didn't matter what he showed her, what she provoked.

She'd rather he strike her than pretend that she meant nothing. That he *felt* nothing.

Her mouth went dry, and she wet her lips. "Did you think you'd scared me off before?"

That had his head coming up again, his hand pausing over the document before him.

She pressed on, moving forward until her hands rested on the edge of the desk. His gaze fixed on her fingers as if they were something foreign and strange.

"Did you think I would frighten so easily?" she continued. "I don't. Your scars don't scare me. Your tragedy will not run me off."

He came to his feet slowly, leaning over the desk as well. "Are you through?"

"No." She had to struggle to swallow because there was a dangerous light in his eyes. She was stoking the fire, prodding the beast. "You might be my guardian, but I am still a grown woman—"

"I'll believe that when I see any evidence of your maturity."

The words stung, but she would not let him see. Instead, she leaned over further. Her gown was low-cut, the fabric stretched taut over her breasts. Parting her lips, she pressed her elbows in, causing her breasts to lift until she was close to spilling out of her bodice.

Her heart raced wildly as he took the bait, his gaze dropping, his eyes darkening. The sheer ravenous hunger in his expression stole her breath and made her legs shake.

But it was the wet heat between her thighs that made her whimper, the sound unbidden and shameful. He dragged his gaze up from her breasts, lingering on her neck and then her lips before meeting her gaze with a look so filled with disdain, it had her stumbling back.

"Is this how you show me how mature you are?" His sneer made her belly twist with humiliation. "You're a child in a grown woman's body, that's what you are. You're playing games you don't fully understand, with consequences you cannot fathom."

Her lungs hitched as he came around the desk in two quick strides, gripping her upper arms as he walked her backward with sure steps. He was so close that his leg came between her thighs, catching in her skirts, like some sort of scandalous dance. He didn't stop until her back brushed up against the wall just beside the door.

Her chest was heaving, her skin tingling with the need for more touches. She wanted him to grip her harder, to push her up against the wall with force. She wanted...no she *needed* to feel his bruising punishment.

She needed to *feel*.

And she needed it more than she needed her pride.

She tilted her head back. "You think I don't understand the consequences?"

Memories came back to haunt her so suddenly, that for a moment, she was lost in them, and she had to blink them away.

She wasn't quick enough because she saw his eyes narrow with curiosity, maybe even concern.

"I know what it is to pay for our sins," she said. "I pay for mine every day."

His brows drew down, and his gaze raked over her face. But she didn't want to talk. She didn't want questions. So, she lifted herself up onto her tiptoes and pressed her mouth to his.

For a moment, he didn't respond. He stilled beneath her kiss like a marble statue. But then all at once, his control gave way and he was ravenous. His mouth claimed hers in a crushing kiss, his hot, firm lips moving over hers with a hunger that made her belly clench and her thighs tremble.

Still gripping her arms, he pressed into her until his hard, massive body was pinning her to the wall. Her mind went blessedly blank as sensations swept through her, hot liquid heat from her breasts down to her toes.

The sensations were overpowering, the rush of heat and

desire so overwhelming, she thought she might drown.

And yet, she wanted even more.

She wouldn't be satisfied until she was completely swept away in this mindless abandon, the first true relief from pain that she'd had in a year.

She moaned as one of his hands came up to cup her breast. Not gentle.

But she didn't want gentle. She wanted to be bruised by his fingers, to feel his touch even after he was gone.

The space between her thighs throbbed, and she was making desperate needy noises in her throat as her hips rocked, trying to find...something. She didn't even know what she needed, only that she was desperate for more.

He pulled back, his breathing labored.

"Lord Foster, I—"

"Go." He scrubbed a hand over his face as he backed away, the fire in his eyes a mix of fury and desire.

That fire made her tremble. "But—"

"Go!" He roared the word, and she ran.

She stumbled into the hallway and back to her room. It wasn't over though, she told herself as she put her hair to rights and called for a maid to mend the bodice which he'd ripped.

As she dressed for dinner, she met her reflection with the ghost of a smile. It was far from her old carefree grin, but far more real than the smile she'd been wearing for the past year.

For the first time in a long time, she felt some hope.

The man could be cruel. He would never speak of love. He didn't even like her.

But that was good.

That was better.

She didn't want romance. She'd learned her lesson there.

When the time came to go back downstairs, she was ready to face him. But he did not come to dinner. She dined alone with Lady Foster, which was a chore unto itself. The woman was so lost in her own isolated world that she hardly made any attempt to speak.

Though tonight she seemed to be making more of an effort, perhaps to make up for the earl's absence. "Are you looking forward to London, dear?"

"Yes, my lady," Philippa said quietly.

She smiled. "Your mother would be so proud."

Spoken so kindly, and yet ice flooded Philippa's veins, and her soup spoon hovered in the air. *She would not be proud. She certainly hadn't been the day she died.*

The day I got her killed.

"You look just like her when she was your age." Lady Foster had continued talking, seemingly oblivious to Philippa's pain.

"I've heard that often," she said, forcing a smile.

But their red hair and green eyes were where the similarities ended. For her mother was an angel—all Christian kindness and an obedient heart.

And Philippa was nothing but trouble.

A fact only the earl seemed to understand. He'd seen it in her right away—not that she'd tried to hide it. He brought it out in her, too. His disapproval and disdain, his threats of punishment…

Oh yes, he knew exactly what she was deep down. And that was liberating in a way. To be seen, for once. To be understood.

Perhaps it was best to stop fighting her true nature, but rather to embrace it. Revel in it.

Drown in her wicked ways until they brought about her own demise.

"I dare say you'll have your pick of a husband," the dowager countess was saying.

Philippa lifted her head. *Husband.* Her lip curled with a sneer at the thought. But this was all part of her punishment. She would not fight it. "I am not so certain," she said in a humble tone. "Aside from your family's gracious patronage, I have no good connections to offer—"

"Nonsense, dear," the dowager countess interrupted. "You're an heiress with a fortune to her name."

A fortune thanks to her parents' untimely death. She sipped her soup. How lucky for her.

"You might not be marriage material for the likes of a duke or an earl, but I daresay you could snare yourself a baronet if you so wished. Perhaps even an impoverished viscount."

Philippa's stomach churned so badly she couldn't eat another bite. A baronet or a viscount… But she was not good enough for an earl, that was what she meant.

Did the old lady see the way she'd been watching Lord Foster?

Was she worried she'd have her heart broken?

The thought nearly made her laugh as she sipped at her soup.

To have one's heart broken, one had to have a heart to break.

CHAPTER FIVE

B ENEDICT WOKE TO the sound of screams.

For a moment, he lay there in bed, his blood running cold and his heart hammering.

It was happening all over again. He was back to that night when his life had come undone.

His fault. All his fault.

He waited for the smell of smoke to invade his nostrils and choke his throat, but instead, he heard another scream, and this time he bolted upright in bed. The world was coming into focus as another shout broke through his sleep-addled haze.

He threw back the covers. There was no smoke. No angry, drunken mistress who'd gone missing in the night.

There was no fire.

But his blood still curdled as another scream pierced the air, chilling with its stark terror. He didn't pause to light a candle or throw on a shirt, and he didn't stop moving until he was at her door, inside her room.

The bedding was twisted around Philippa as she tossed and turned, her eyes squeezed shut and her features tight with fear.

His heart slammed against his ribcage as she rolled toward him, muttering in her sleep.

She was asleep. His shoulders slumped. She was having a nightmare.

Her muttering turned to whimpers, and his heart responded again. Not with a kick of alarm but something far worse. Something rare.

It ached.

The organ squeezed tight as he moved toward her, his chest growing more constricted with each step. Sitting on the edge of the bed, he hesitated before touching her arm. "Philippa," he said gently.

She turned toward his voice, rolling toward his body like a frightened little creature seeking warmth.

Air left him in a rush as her face came into the moonlight.

Stunning. Her cheekbones were highlighted by the glow, her lips kissed by it. Her hair was braided, but long locks had been freed during her tossing and turning, and one was matted to her temple by sweat.

She whimpered again, and his heart broke.

He hadn't known it could break any more than it already had, but there it was. "Philippa." He shook her gently.

She moaned as she stirred.

"Philippa, love, it's only a dream."

A nightmare, rather. Of what? What haunted this sweet girl's dreams?

And yes, she was sweet. Despite her taunting earlier, or maybe because of it, he knew that much to be true. There'd been a vulnerability there in her eyes and in her kiss, desperation that had underlain her bold actions and her sharp tongue.

His gaze fell to her lips, and the memory of that kiss nearly crushed him.

Mistake. The kiss had been a mistake.

"No," she said, so clearly it startled him. "No, Mother, please. Father!"

With that last sharp cry, she sat upright.

"You're all right, love," he said softly, with as much gentleness as he could muster.

It didn't come naturally to him. Kindness and softness were

not a part of this family's makeup. A fact he'd always known but which had only been made more clear this past year.

They did not do weeping and grieving, but rather resentment and guilt.

Philippa's wide eyes blinked open. As he watched her wake, her eyes focused as she realized where she was...

He saw it clear as day. That moment when the new life settles in and when reality returns and grief sweeps in all over again.

Another day to survive. That was what he saw in her gaze. The same sinking horror he'd felt every morning since the fire.

She swallowed hard as she turned to face him. "Lord Foster?"

His lips twitched at the confusion in her voice. His shaft twitched, too, at that breathless quality in her voice. Husky from sleep and her body covered by only the thin cotton of her nightdress.

"Are you all right?" He ordered himself not to look down. Not to drink in the sight of her.

She was not his to look upon. Not like that.

"I..." She shook her head, a hand coming up to touch her temple. "It was a nightmare." Her gaze flicked up to meet his. "Did I wake you? I'm sorry."

"Don't apologize." It came out too harsh, and she flinched.

Bloody hell, he wasn't good at these things. He thought for a moment to call for his mother, but then again... He might not be good at giving comfort, but his mother was far worse.

"I...I..." She cast a glance around as if the words might be nearby. And then, to his horror, she burst out in tears.

He reached out and pulled her into his arms. "Shh, it's all right, child."

"I'm not a child," she mumbled in a high, watery voice against his shoulder.

His lips twitched again. "No, of course not."

And she wasn't. This much was clear to him. She might have an innocent look about her, but she was no child. She was soon to be married, after all. And beyond that, she'd been through a tragedy that made a person grow up, whether they were ready or not.

And then there were her curves.

He grit his teeth, trying not to notice.

There was nothing childlike about the way she fit against his chest. She wrapped her arms around his neck and clung to him in a way that made it impossible to breathe.

Desire swept through him, hard and fierce at the feel of her soft breasts crushing against his muscles. The scent of her was intoxicating—so fresh, so floral and sweet.

"I shouldn't be here." The words were strangled like they'd been ripped out of her.

He pulled back, trying to see her face, but she buried her head in the crook of his neck.

Her tears wet his bare skin.

Hell, he didn't even have a shirt on. Thank God it was dark in here, or he'd give her nightmares all over again with the sight of the burns and scars that covered his neck and chest.

He wrapped his arms around her and stroked her back. "Of course you should be here," he said, his low voice echoing oddly in the quiet of her dark bedroom. "My mother is your godmother, this is exactly where you ought to be—"

"No, I shouldn't be *here*." Her voice was ravaged with pain. "I shouldn't be alive."

She shook her head, pressing away from him, but he stopped her, cupping her face in his hands, a clawing sensation in his chest making speech impossible.

I shouldn't be alive.

He knew the feeling well. He thought it most every day. Survivor's guilt, his friend Hayden had called it. A natural reaction to having survived a tragedy when those you love did not. Made worse for him since it was his fault that the fire started. He'd brought his mistress here, enjoying the fact that her scandalous presence would irritate his father and infuriate his stick-in-the-mud brother. He'd been the one who'd gotten too drunk, who'd ignored his temperamental mistress and her ridiculous demands.

Tomorrow, he'd told himself that night. He'd deal with her money-grabbing, melodramatic tirades in the morning.

But Francesca hadn't wanted to wait. She'd been even more intoxicated than he'd been—he realized that belatedly. It came back to him in the days that followed the tragedy. He could remember vividly how her eyes had sparkled—and the vacant crazed look he'd seen there.

It had been something more than alcohol at work. Opium, maybe. Perhaps something else.

Not that it mattered now.

None of it mattered now because the damage was already done. He still didn't know exactly how she'd done it or why. If it was an accident or an act of spite. The fact that she'd been in his brother's room made him think she'd taken her chances with the older brother. An act of revenge on Benedict after he'd spurned her.

He shook his head now, his gaze still fixed on Philippa's. Her eyes were distant, dazed. It seemed she, too, was lost in the past, and her gaze was filled with such torment, it was impossible not to feel it, too.

I shouldn't be alive.

Oh yes, he understood the sentiment all too well. But coming from her—from those sweet lips and the innocent eyes. She was no sheltered child, but she wasn't nearly as wicked as she'd like to believe either.

She was…well, perhaps not *good*. Good was too tepid a word for a woman like Philippa. But she was pure. Deep down, beneath her mischief and her tumultuous emotions, there was a light in her that she could not hide.

She might act the part of a seductive siren, but he'd seen enough of her to know that what drove her was not evil nor malicious. Just human.

The girl was lost. She was seeking something.

Something she seemed to think she might find in his arms.

He huffed with bitter amusement. Perhaps she was seeking to punish herself. For surely any sane woman would see intimacy with a monster as torture.

He stroked a thumb over her cheek, wiping away a tear. Her lower lip trembled.

"You deserve to be alive, Philippa."

Her eyes focused on his. He could see that she wanted to believe him, but then her face crumpled. "You don't know what I've done."

He shook his head. "I don't need to. Just like I don't need to have known your parents to know that they wouldn't want you throwing your life away because you are grieving."

And precisely what she'd do if she kept up her salacious behavior.

"It's not just grief." She tugged her head away, out of his grip. "You wouldn't understand."

"Wouldn't I?"

It was like looking in a mirror.

"Philippa, don't do this to yourself."

She sniffed.

His hands itched to reach for her again, but the way he was straining against his breeches made him all too aware of the danger here. He shifted to leave. "Get some sleep."

The words felt far too insufficient, but he had no idea how to help her.

He couldn't even help himself. Why did he think he could help her?

He went to stand but stilled at the feel of her small, soft hand covering his. "Wait."

For a long moment, all he could hear was their breathing. Hers was short and choppy, and her grip tightened on his. "Don't leave me."

She turned wide, tear-filled eyes in his direction, and...he was done for. Blast. A grown man taken down at the knees by one teary look.

Oh, how his friends would take pleasure in this. He could practically hear Raff and Hayden laughing now.

He fought against the heat coiling in his loins as her scent wrapped around him. He couldn't stay. Sitting here so close to her, in such an intimate setting—this was already taxing his limited powers of restraint. He used his free hand to try and gently remove her hand from his. "You need sleep, love. The nightmare is over—"

Her high, humorless burst of laughter made him pause.

"The nightmare is not over," she said with a bitter smile that made his chest clench. "My nightmare will never be over so long as I live."

She was in earnest, and pity temporarily won out over lust. He saw such loneliness in her eyes. Such unbearable pain. He reached for her and pulled her close, making a shushing noise against her temple as she burrowed into him as if she belonged there.

He closed his eyes, inhaling her scent and letting himself revel in the feel of her soft, sweet heat.

But then she was shifting, and he felt it. Her lips against his chest, her breath hot on his already overheated skin.

He jerked back as if burnt, gripping her by the elbows to push her away. "What are you doing?"

Her lips were parted, but there was no taunting smirk. Only desperation. A plea that tugged at his heart, even as his mind set off a warning bell.

This way trouble lies, it seemed to say.

As if he didn't know that. This girl had been nothing but trouble since she'd arrived.

"Philippa, we mustn't," he said, but the words trailed off in a groan when she reached for him, her slim fingers tracing over his arms and chest. Her gaze was riveted as it raked over his left side, cataloging every scar, and he waited for it—some sign of revulsion.

Instead, she wetted her lips. "You've been through so much pain."

His grunt was hardly eloquent, but it was all he could muster when all the blood in his body had rushed to his cock. His bollocks tightened with need, and while he knew he had to end it, the feel of her touch, so gentle and so curious... He couldn't bring himself to pull away.

How long had it been since anyone had touched him like this?

It had been more than six months since he'd slept with Francesca, but it had been much longer than that since anyone had touched him with such tenderness.

It choked his throat and made speech impossible.

"You're so hard," she said. For a second, he thought she'd seen his erection, and his shaft answered her by growing even more swollen. But then she continued in a whisper. "All over, so hard. Inside and out. I want to be like that."

He gripped her wrist, stilling her hand when it dipped down to touch the flat planes above his naval. "That's enough."

Her gaze intensified, something in the air around her sparked and heated.

He could see the change in her, but he could also see what caused it. Desperation.

His stomach turned even as his erection begged him to take advantage. She didn't want him, not really. She just needed a distraction. Relief from her pain.

He could understand it, but it still left a sickening taste in his mouth.

Her free hand reached down so quickly, he didn't have a chance to stop her, and he hissed when her fingers brushed over his hard member.

Her gaze shot up to his, wide and questioning. "Did I hurt you?"

He choked on a laugh of disbelief. Had she hurt him?

She was killing him with her touch.

When he didn't answer, she kept exploring, her fingers quick and light as she stroked his length through the fabric.

His heart pounded, harsh and fierce. He should push her away. He should stand and walk away.

That was what his brain said. His cock had another view on the matter.

She wants this, it seemed to say. *Give the girl what she craves.*

He swallowed hard and groaned when she grew brave and cupped her hand over his length, giving him a light squeeze.

"This isn't right," he said. But even he could hear how labored his breathing was, and he couldn't bring himself to move as she hitched herself up onto her knees, hastily tugging at the bodice of her nightdress until it was falling down around her shoulders.

"Philippa, no," he said.

But it was too late. Her pert, round breasts were there on full display.

"Christ," he whispered. He'd never seen anything more beautiful. She sat up straight and proud, her gaze open, and with just a hint of doubt as if waiting for his reaction. Her skin was silky pale in the moon's glow.

The sight of her hard, dark peaks made his mouth water. "So beautiful, love," he murmured. "So perfect."

The words were the reminder that he needed.

He wasn't the man he'd once been. She was every inch the beautiful young lady, but he wasn't the handsome, dashing earl who could make a woman wet with a heated look. He was broken and scarred, his inner demons on display for all the world to see.

It nearly killed him, but he shook his head and looked away. "You'll make your husband a happy man someday, Philippa. But this is not for me."

She lunged forward, wrapping her arms around his neck. The move had her hard nipples scraping against his chest, and his palms burned with the need to touch her.

He curled them into fists at his side instead.

"You're an innocent," he said. It came out sounding like an accusation.

"I'm not," she whispered against his neck.

Her words had him blinking in surprise.

"I'm not," she said again, this time rubbing her perfect tits over his chest like a cat asking to be stroked. They both moaned at the sweet friction of her soft curves against his hardness. She was straddling his thighs now, her nightdress bunching up around her curvy, smooth thighs, and her tight little cunny so close to his cock, it took everything he had not to grab her hips and drag her down on top of him to grind his hardness against her heat.

"I'm not a virgin," she whispered in his ear, her breath hot and sweet.

He groaned. She was temptation itself, rubbing against him and pleading to be taken.

Jesus, how was he supposed to deny himself this?

His bollocks were achingly tight as he brought his hands to her hips…and set her away from him. It took every ounce of his willpower, but he set her away with a determined movement.

"Not tonight, love," he said.

Not ever.

She'd hate herself in the morning when she saw his face, remembered who he was. It was that thought that gave him the strength to pull away.

But she leaned forward and pressed her lips to his, no doubt trying to spark the same unrestrained passion she'd unleashed in him earlier that day.

It wouldn't work. That kiss had been a mistake. He wouldn't lose control again.

But he couldn't control a growl of need when she caught his hand and settled it over her right breast, the hard nub of her nipple pressing into his palm.

He lost vision for a second, the need was that intense.

"Please," she whispered against his lips, her hand covering his as she held it over her breast. "Please. I want to forget."

There was that desperation again. She wasn't seeking him out because of desire or attraction, merely desperation. He understood that—the need to escape one's torturous thoughts, the memories, the regrets.

He understood it, but it still cut like a knife and forced him back to reality.

He stood with a sharp exhale, tugging his hand from hers with jerky movements. "Get some sleep, Philippa. We leave for London at first light."

Chapter Six

THE TRIP TO London was brutal.

Not because the roads were terrible. Just the company. Lady Foster had opted to ride in a separate carriage with her lady's maid, which left Philippa alone with the earl.

He seemed content to ignore her existence, preferring instead to brood.

She crossed her arms and looked out the window with a sigh. "Don't you ever tire of brooding gloominess?"

He shot her a withering look.

But when his gaze dipped to her breasts, she smiled. He hadn't forgotten. He might be content to pretend last night hadn't happened, but she could sense his desire. She could see it in his eyes every time he looked her way.

Her skin burned whenever she thought of the way he'd pushed her away, striding out the door without so much as a backward glance. It was humiliating. And shocking. Who would have thought the big, bad wicked earl she'd heard so much about would be a gentleman?

His silence this morning was killing her though. She could handle his disdain. She rather enjoyed his anger. But ignoring her? This was insufferable.

"Aren't you worried about being alone in a carriage with me?" she asked, mostly to break the silence.

His gaze slowly moved over to her as if he'd forgotten she was there. "Why would I worry? I am your guardian. You are my ward. There's nothing scandalous going on here."

One brow arched slightly.

Imperious, smug arse.

She narrowed her eyes in annoyance, and his lips twitched with amusement in return.

She tilted her head to the side to study him. Oddly enough, when he was acting all high and mighty like this, it was almost easy to forget about his scars. They were still there in full view, of course. Perhaps she'd gotten used to the sight of his mutilated skin. When he wasn't glowering and brooding, she could imagine exactly what he'd looked like before. Exactly who he'd been.

"You must have been an incorrigible rake," she said suddenly.

"Pardon?"

"My mother told me stories about you." She ignored his glare and folded her hands primly. "I was led to believe you were utterly wicked. The very devil himself."

"Were you?" he murmured.

He didn't protest. If anything, she thought she caught wry amusement in the quirk of his lips.

"Oh yes. Your mother sent my mother regular correspondence, and my favorite part was when she went on at length about your reckless deeds and your roguish behavior."

He grunted at that.

"So, you can see why I'm so offended that you would not ravish me."

He sighed, looking away as if bored.

But a glance down at his lap had her smirking. He might act bored, even put out by her bad manners and scandalous talk. But the reminder of last night's embrace was enough to make his manhood visible.

She bit her lip as it seemed to grow beneath her gaze.

My, but he was…large.

Granted, she had little to go on by way of comparison. But

she knew quite well where that was supposed to fit, and she squirmed uncomfortably in her seat as she tried to imagine that large, hard member thrusting inside her.

Oh goodness. Perhaps she shouldn't imagine. Her pulse was far too fast, and there was hot wetness between her thighs that was so intense it was painful.

"Stop." His growl was a curt command. "I know you mean to scandalize me with your behavior, but it will not work, you know."

"What won't?" Her chin came up in defiance.

He leaned forward. "You're hell-bent on ruining yourself, that much is clear. What I don't understand is what you hope to gain."

She stared at him for a long moment. Disappointment poked at her belly. She'd thought he'd understood. But no. He didn't understand at all if he thought she was hoping to obtain something.

Couldn't he see she was trying to destroy it? The last of her pride, the remains of her good name. For a year now she'd had to suffer a fate worse than death.

Sympathy.

Pity.

Her parents' friends had swarmed around her, and even when she'd tried to explain—to confess that it was all her fault—no one would listen.

No one would punish her the way she deserved.

They just showered her with more kindness and threw platitudes her way about how it wasn't her fault. It was an accident.

They knew nothing.

Anger shot through her at Lord Foster's penetrating gaze. And now he was no better.

He sighed. "We'll find you a match in London. A good man who'll—"

"Or you could just marry me," she said.

He stared at her until she laughed. She hadn't truly meant it. She'd just wanted to see his response, and his chilling glare had been worth it.

Far better than his feigned nonchalance.

"Ah, yes," she continued. "But, of course, I'm not good enough for an earl such as yourself." She shook her head. "Whatever would your mother say?"

"It's not my mother I worry about," he said.

She frowned. What did that mean?

He looked out the window.

"You do need to marry, do you not?"

Silence. Of course he did.

"You must be able to have your pick," she continued. "After all, you are an earl."

He glanced over then, his gaze withering. "Is that supposed to be a jab?"

"What do you mean?"

With a quick wave of his hand, he gestured to the burned side of his face. "This. You think any woman wants this?"

Her heart twisted and, for a moment, she was rendered speechless by guilt. This was the second time he'd assumed she was mocking him for his injuries. "They're not so bad as you think."

He scoffed, and she felt her cheeks begin to burn. Dratted man, she hated blushing. But she hated it even more that he thought she'd been cruel.

To herself, yes. To him...no.

He might not be the warmest fellow, but he'd done nothing to hurt her. If anything, he'd been doing too good of a job protecting her honor.

"I mean it," she said. "Once you get used to them, they're no longer distracting. And..." She swallowed as his dark, heavy gaze fell on her like a weight. "And it's easy to see how handsome you were." She gestured toward the unmarred side. "Strong jawline and handsome features... The scars are easy to overlook."

His eyes bore into her. No doubt he was trying to see if she was serious.

"Still, all the same," she continued, trying for a breezy tone to cover her discomfort. "I'm certain London society is not easy to maneuver with all the whispers about what happened that night."

He flinched.

She opened her mouth and shut it. It was none of her concern. And yet... She couldn't stop thinking about the things he'd said last night. The way he'd seemed to understand her anguish in a way others had not. "Was it your fault?"

His gaze didn't waver. "Yes."

Her lungs contracted. She waited for more, but that was all he would say, it seemed. "Is that why your mother..." She flailed a hand uselessly. *Is that why she so obviously hates you? Is that why you're never in the same room without caustic comments and thinly veiled barbs?*

She settled for, "Is that why she didn't wish to ride in this carriage?"

A hint of wry, bitter amusement lit his eyes as if he'd heard all she hadn't said. "Probably."

She winced, uncertain what to say to that.

But then he added, "It's for the best, though."

Something about the way he said it felt less guarded than usual. She arched a brow. "Because if she were here, she'd be criticizing you?"

He tilted his head to the side. "No. Because she snores."

A laugh bubbled out of her, and she clapped a hand over her mouth. Her heart fluttered dangerously when her laughter was met with a smile. An honest to goodness smile that formed creases around his mouth and made his eyes crinkle and...oh my.

It was very easy indeed to overlook the scars when he smiled at her like that.

"She sleeps on long journeys, I take it?" she managed.

"Mmm." He cast a glance out the window. "If you're very quiet, you may be able to hear her."

She giggled again, and his gaze met hers, soft and indulgent.

That look made her warm all over, in a way that was mostly

pleasant. Rather like when she'd come inside and stood before a fire after being out in the cold.

The warmth was welcome even as it stung.

She blinked in surprise at the unexpected feelings he stirred in her chest. This was a first. A first since her parents' death, at least, that someone's kindness didn't make her feel even colder than usual and walled off from the world around her.

No, his rare displays of tenderness and affection caused an entirely different reaction inside of her.

Perhaps that was because when he looked at her, he saw *her*—not some pathetic orphan or an innocent young girl to be coddled. There was no leniency and no pity when he spoke to her. His air was commanding, and she knew without a doubt how he would be like as a husband.

Demanding. Stern. He was a man who ruled over his domain with a firm hand.

She wiggled in her seat. And oh, how she ached to feel that firm hand.

She swallowed a wave of embarrassment at the thought. He brought this out in her, and she couldn't explain it. But as he watched her squirm, his eyes dark and hot, her mind went rogue again. Imagining what life would be like as his wife.

He'd be stern, yes. But affectionate, too, at times.

Her heart did a flip when she recalled the way he'd held her the night before.

"Where did that wicked little mind of yours wander?" he asked softly.

The low growl made her shiver, and she squeezed her legs together tight.

I was imagining being your wife.

Definitely not something she could admit. She'd been teasing when she'd brought it up. He was an earl, for heaven's sake. And she, a foreigner. He did not need her fortune, and while her mother would have delighted at the idea of her snaring a title, she didn't deserve that sort of triumph.

She didn't deserve the "good man" he promised to find her either.

And honestly, as she met his dark gaze and felt this heavy weight in her breasts and belly—an effect he and he alone seemed to have on her—she wasn't sure she wanted any other man.

The idea had barely even formed before she blurted it out. "Take me as your mistress."

His brows shot up. "What?"

She straightened. The idea was a good one.

He sighed like she was some exasperating chit. "You're a gently bred young lady, Philippa. I don't know why you're so intent on destruction, but I will not allow it."

Too late, though. She'd already destroyed her life. The only course left was to find a way to survive the long years to come.

She'd already ruled out taking her own life. It was too easy a way out.

But she didn't deserve a family, nor a household of her own. Certainly not the blood money that had come in the form of an inheritance.

The idea took hold, and she grasped onto it, feeling more alive now than she had in ages. Because now she had a plan.

"Don't you want me?" She bit her lip, giving him her best coy look.

He rolled his eyes. "It's not a matter of want—"

"If you want me, then take me," she said. She threw it out like a challenge and watched with breathless fascination as his eyes darkened. If she were to straddle his lap again, would he be hard between her thighs?

Most definitely.

A little push, another nudge. She drew a finger over her collarbone and down, dragging his gaze down along her breasts as well.

He wanted her. And that was enough. If she tempted him long enough, if she pushed him to the edge—

Yes. That was what she wanted. She wanted to rile his passion, his anger, his stern command. She wanted to lose herself in his punishment. She wanted to be taken, hard and ruthless. To be used and abandoned...

It was wrong and twisted, this need inside of her—but she knew what she needed to do. It was such a fitting punishment. Such a well-deserved end.

"It's not going to happen, pet," he said, his voice a low drawl, so very sanctimonious.

"Would you like to place a wager?" she teased in a sing-song voice.

"If you don't care who you marry, I'll choose the man for you," he said, his jaw tight.

"And when you do, I'll explain to this man that I've already been ruined." She tried to smile, but it turned into a sad smirk. "I'll tell him I'm spoiled goods, and this fine gentleman of yours will undoubtedly cast me off."

He stared at her long and hard, his jaw working as he considered her. The words seemed to be torn out of him at last. "Who was he? Who was this man who took your innocence?"

She met his gaze evenly. "Why? Does it matter?"

He leaned forward, his eyes so dark she saw his inner hell. "I will kill him."

She swallowed. It wasn't an idle threat. It was a vow.

She dragged her gaze away. "Then I suppose I can never tell you his name." She forced a smile. "I shouldn't want to lose my lover to the gallows."

"I'm not your—" He cut himself off with a harsh curse. "You're playing with fire, little girl." He leaned over, and she could feel the heat of his breath on her cheek. "You're going to get hurt."

"Impossible," she whispered.

His gaze flickered over her as he tried to understand.

But if he hadn't figured it out by now, he never would.

You cannot hurt what's already dead.

And her heart? Her heart had been reduced to a pile of ash a year ago.

CHAPTER SEVEN

B ENEDICT NEVER THOUGHT he'd find himself relieved to be in society. He couldn't have fathomed a day when he was glad to be at a ball, of all things, rather than safely tucked away in his own home.

But here he was. Relieved as hell to be surrounded by the same people whose whispers and stares had driven him out of London only weeks before.

"Another drink?" his friend the Marquess of Hayden offered.

Benedict threw back the drink Hayden handed him, hoping that might help to assuage the unceasing frustration he was currently trying to avoid by attending this tedious soiree. But tedious or not, at least he wasn't trapped at home with Phillipa.

His London townhome had become a torturous den of private moments alone with his bloody ward from hell.

His mother was no help. She'd kept herself occupied with her friends or hidden away in her private quarters.

Which left no one but him to entertain Philippa. No one but him to keep her in line.

No one at all to save him from her ceaseless temptations.

Just this morning she'd cornered him alone in his study, her gown off her shoulders as she'd described in excruciating details just how good it had felt when he'd kissed her.

"Will you do it again?" she'd taunted, her hands on his chest as she pressed herself against him. "Please, my lord."

How was a man supposed to withstand that temptation? It was too much.

"I need to find her a husband," he said to Hayden when the drink was drained.

Hayden was smirking at him. "She's gotten under your skin, has she?"

Benedict grunted an affirmative, his gaze already seeking her out again. His mother had finally stepped up in her role of chaperone for tonight's occasion, and he'd found some blessed relief as the dowager countess had whisked her off to make introductions.

But now even that hint of relief was gone because he spotted her. It was difficult to miss a beauty like Philippa in this crowd. She seemed to glow with life and vitality amidst the stuffy, tedious people.

And then there was her beauty, of course. Not only did her pale gown and radiant smile attract his attention, it had a veritable crush of gentlemen surrounding her, eagerly awaiting an introduction.

"Word has spread about her fortune," Hayden mused. The infamously handsome marquess with the deceptive charm shot him a sidelong glance. "You'll need to be on your guard against fortune hunters."

Another grunt of acknowledgment, which turned into a growl as he watched a young, handsome, familiar gentleman approach. A man they knew without a doubt was after a fortune.

"Oh hell," Hayden muttered, craning his neck. "Is she talking to…Foley?"

The disdain in his voice was clear. They'd both heard about the way Foley had tried to steal their friend Raff's new bride from him. It hadn't worked, but they were all too aware that he was not the affable, harmless fellow they'd all believed.

He let out a relieved exhale when Foley was replaced by an old bore whose name he couldn't place. There was nothing about this man that would tempt Philippa. He was old enough to be her grandfather, and he knew from experience his breath reeked of fish and ale.

He tore his gaze away. What was he doing finding fault with these gentlemen? The sooner he got her off his hands, the better. Right?

He turned to find Hayden watching him closely. "What?" he snapped.

Hayden's smirk tested his already low patience. "I don't believe I've ever seen you so...flustered."

Benedict jerked back. "I am not flustered. I'm...I'm..."

Hayden arched his brows.

Benedict turned away with a sigh. "I'm at my wit's end."

"She's that aggravating, is she?" he asked. "What, does she nag you like a mother? Harp on you like a shrew? Berate you for drinking?"

Benedict ignored his friend, who seemed much too amused by his personal hell.

"I know," Hayden said, his gaze following Benedict's, which had strayed back to the red-haired beauty on the far side of the room. "She forced you to come out of that cave you've been hiding in this past year."

Benedict spared him a glare. She had at that. Though her methods were not what Hayden could ever guess. But her tempting and her taunting had not only driven him to distraction, they'd driven him outside, into stables...and now back to bloody society.

When Benedict didn't take the bait, Hayden continued. "Perhaps I should court her."

That did it. Benedict spun toward him, gripping his glass so hard he feared it might shatter. "You wouldn't."

Hayden's smile was sweet. Too innocent. Benedict had known his friend since their school days and knew far better to believe he was anything close to innocent.

"Why not?" Hayden asked with a shrug. "That's what Raff

has us doing this season, isn't it?" He arched his brows. "I believe our esteemed duke made us both take a vow that this season we would each choose our bride."

Benedict grunted, half amused and half irritated at the reminder of their highhanded old friend.

"You for obvious reasons," Hayden said with a gesture in Benedict's direction.

The obvious reason was that Benedict had never been meant to be the earl. The reminder settled on his shoulders like a dead weight. It was always there, the knowledge that this was not his life. That he'd stolen it from his father and brother.

"You can't go on with just you and your mother like that." Hayden's voice was unusually serious, and Benedict gave a huff of agreement.

It was no secret that he and his mother were only making each other more miserable. Not that he blamed her, necessarily. It was his fault that her life had been ruined, after all.

"You need a wife more than anyone," Hayden said.

"And yet here you are," Benedict muttered, more to change the topic than anything.

Hayden chuckled, looking around him. "And yet, here I am. I do need an heir, I can't deny it." His expression grew mischievous. "And your ward is certainly a tempting option."

"Don't even think of it," Benedict growled. Rage was real, and it coiled in his gut.

Hayden only chuckled. He'd never been afraid of Benedict, not even back when they were children.

"Why not?" Hayden asked.

"Because she's not meant to be a marchioness, for one," he said, the words tasting sour on his tongue. But it was true. She might be an heiress and have friends in high places, but she did not have the family connections to make her a viable option. Not to mention, she'd been raised Catholic. "Your father would come back from the grave to murder you."

Hayden's smirk was bitter. "All the more reason then." He

lifted a glass. "To vengeance."

Benedict ignored him. No need to rise to Hayden's insufferable bait. The conversation had to come to an end anyway as his ward was drawing near, a sweet, small smile curving her lips as her gaze met his.

Hayden had already been introduced, and he wasted no time ingratiating himself with Philippa with compliments and small talk.

Benedict knew his friend had no serious interest in her. But he likely would if he got to know her. One whiff of the dangerous, mischievous, wicked girl beneath this innocent flower facade and he'd be all over her.

Hayden might have to marry well, but he had no interest in demure debutantes and proper ladies. In fact, that was everything he didn't want in life.

Benedict inched closer to Philippa. Hayden would love nothing more than to find himself a rebellious, seductive little hoyden.

But there was no way. He loved Hayden like a brother— more than his own brother, God rest his soul. But the thought of his rakish friend seducing Philippa made his insides revolt. Hayden would not know—not at first, at least. He would see the pretense, believe her worldly, devil-may-care act, and not realize until too late that it covered a wounded soul, an innocent heart.

There was pain there beneath Philippa's outrageous flirting, and he didn't trust anyone else to see it. It took pain to recognize pain, and—

And what was he thinking? That he was the only one who could understand her? The only one who could give her what she needed?

The thought sent the room spinning about him, and for a moment, he forgot where he was and why.

Until his no-good friend called Benedict's focus back to the scene before him with his hearty laughter and overly attentive air.

The cad was blatantly flirting with the girl.

He glared at Hayden when his friend donned his most charming smile—the one that had been known to make young ladies swoon. "Would you care to dance?" Hayden asked.

Benedict growled, which had Hayden casting him an amused glance.

"I'm afraid this dance has already been claimed," Philippa said, her voice high and sweet. If he didn't know better, he'd say she truly was an innocent flower. A sweet little lamb who needed to be protected.

She held up her dance card to Benedict, a glimmer of laughter in her eyes. "You are my next dance partner. See? It says so right here."

He gritted his teeth at the sight of her handwriting spelling out his name.

Incorrigible little chit.

And yet, a hint of laughter was brewing in his belly, itching to break free.

Incorrigible, yes. But no one could deny she was persistent. Brazen, too.

And perhaps this was why she was so bloody intriguing. One moment she was a vulnerable, fragile creature whom he longed to protect. The next she was a meddlesome, mischievous little whirlwind. And then of course there were those moments when she was nothing less than a siren intent on leading him to his doom.

Philippa batted her lashes at Hayden with a sweet smile. "But I would be honored to dance with you in the future, my lord."

Benedict scowled down at her. Honored, indeed. One would never guess she'd whispered another offer to Benedict just before they'd departed the carriage earlier. Once more she'd asked to be his mistress.

The bloody irritating little minx. She knew he'd say no—he always said no—but she likely also knew his mind would be filled with lewd thoughts about her for the remainder of the evening.

He wasn't sure which was more infuriating—that she was offering to debase herself by becoming a lowly mistress when any man would be happy to take her as a wife—or that he was so sorely tempted to take her up on it.

It was a mistake, of course. He'd never do it. But there were times he was so addled with lust at the sight of her, he couldn't remember why.

He made a mental list now as her gaze caught his, and she led the way through the crowd toward the music.

His mother, for one. She'd never forgive him for ruining her dearest friend's reputation. Not that she'd ever forgive him for what he'd done to their family anyhow.

But there was his own honor to consider, as well. He'd never forgive himself for destroying an innocent just because he couldn't control his desire.

And of course, the reasons he'd rattled off to Hayden. It would be outrageous for a gentleman of their ranking to marry a lady such as she. It could be done, of course. But not without a fair amount of scandal.

Since when have you run from scandal?

Since he'd inherited the title—after his reputation was already thoroughly damaged. Too little too late, his father would have said.

In truth, Benedict had actively sought out scandal in the past. But that was before. He was an earl now, and if he couldn't undo the mistakes that led to his family's tragedy, he could at the very least do the title justice and not make a mess of it like he had in his former life.

Philippa smiled up at him expectantly as the strains of a waltz began.

He held out an arm but added a sigh for good measure. Best not to let her think she'd won.

Except, they both knew she had the moment he drew her into his arms.

"What are you thinking?" she asked after a silence as she moved gracefully to the music.

"I was thinking I'd been mistaken in believing you are a siren," he said.

Her brows arched in question, amusement in her gaze as she waited for him to continue.

"You are clearly a witch."

She giggled. An honest to goodness giggle that was so delightfully innocent and untutored, it had his own lips twitching in turn.

More than that, for the first time all evening, the knot of frustration was easing in his gut...if not his breeches. He was half-erect just touching her waist and feeling her gloved hand in his.

There was no other explanation but witchcraft.

Whenever she was near, he felt desire. That was a given. But being with her here in the midst of a crowd...well, he *still* felt desire. Lust burned under his skin, and he was acutely aware of the way her lips were parted as she gazed at him. Painfully in tune with the rise and fall of those luscious breasts that he couldn't stop imagining.

But the more shocking realization was that he was relaxed. In pain from wanting her, of course, but the dread and torture he'd felt only weeks before when he'd first arrived in town to search for a wife alongside Raff and Hayden?

That was gone.

Perhaps he was just too distracted keeping an eye on her to pay attention to the stares and whispers. Yes, that was it. She kept his thoughts too well occupied. Lord knew he hadn't given a single thought to finding a bride tonight. How could he look for a potential wife when this girl now governed his every thought?

"Have you chosen the gentleman you wish for me to marry?" she asked suddenly. An impish grin curved her lips.

He frowned at the mere thought of another man taking what she kept offering to him.

She smiled, and the smugness there said she knew exactly how green with envy her comment had made him.

He ought to do what he'd first threatened. Take her over her knee for teasing him like this. She had to know that the thought of any other man touching her made him boil over with rage.

Not that he'd let that stop him from finding her a good match. It was his duty to do so.

You could marry me.

He tugged her closer in his arms. Little minx. Speaking of marriage like it meant nothing. Talking about being a man's mistress as if she didn't care where she ended up in life.

"Why are you glaring at me like that?" she asked with a little pout. "I've been on my best behavior this evening."

"So you have." He gave her a wry smile. "That's why I'm watching you so closely."

"So suspicious." She laughed. "I'm watching you closely, too, you know."

He arched a brow, noting with fascination the way her cheeks pinkened, and her whole being seemed to come alive with dancing.

He'd never been much for dancing himself. But it was clear that she enjoyed it. And dancing with Philippa was…not horrible. Not nearly as bad as a trembling debutante too scared to meet his gaze.

"You've been watching me, hmm?" He struggled to hold her gaze and not let it dip down to the tempting cleavage on full display.

Christ, he wished he didn't know just how perfect her breasts looked in the moonlight. The sight would haunt him for life.

"I don't like the way people look at you."

The suddenness of her statement had him blinking down at her. "Pardon?"

She tilted her head to the side with a little pout that made his manhood stiffen. His horrid mind showed him instantly what those lips would look like wrapped around his hard length.

"I just… How can you stand it?" she asked, thick emotions tingeing her tone.

He continued to stare. No one had talked about this with him. Not his mother, obviously. They rarely talked. But not even

Raff or Hayden had acknowledged the change that had occurred.

He'd always been a wild rebel, slightly on the outskirts of good society because of his reckless demeanor, but always welcomed in good society because of his friendship with a marquess and a duke.

Now he was welcomed because he was an earl, but he'd never felt less like he belonged.

"I don't like it," she said again, a sulk in her tone that made him want to pull her close to kiss her for caring...or maybe spank that little bottom for sounding like a spoiled brat.

He grew painfully hard at that thought. He'd spank her until she was wet and moaning and begging for him to take her.

"Don't you agree?" she asked.

He cleared his throat. "Pardon?"

She sighed. "That it's wrong. The way they stare at you like you're an outcast—"

"I am an outcast."

"No," she shot back. "You're an earl."

He grunted. "I shouldn't be."

"But you are."

He swallowed a groan as her brow furrowed with a frown, and she leaned into him.

God, but it would be so easy to tug her closer still. To crush her against him, heedless of all the prying stares around them. To feel her breasts and dip his head and—

"You're an earl, and it's not right that they treat you like this while I...while they..." She shook her head, and his gut clenched with worry. She glanced away, but not before he'd seen a flicker of that deep-seated pain in her eyes. The haunted look that called up her words from the other night and had cold terror sliding through his veins. *I shouldn't be here.*

"While you what?" he demanded.

She shook her head. "Never mind."

"No, what is it?" Frustration made his voice gruffer than usual. There was a piece he was missing with Philippa. She kept it buried, and that pained him. It physically caused him pain when she hid away from him. Like right now. For a moment she'd spoken impulsively, and genuinely, without the trumped-up air of seduction or the childish taunting.

She'd spoken like a woman spoke to a man she respected. To a friend, even.

He tipped his head down further. "Tell me, Philippa."

"Or what?" She smirked up at him. Just like that, she was hiding behind her shield.

He ignored the question. She wanted to flirt and banter.

"Tell me," he growled. "How are they treating you that has you so upset?"

"I'm not upset."

He didn't bother to argue. Protectiveness was a frighteningly powerful emotion. "If anyone has slighted you, I'll—"

"They haven't," she huffed. "Don't you see? That's the problem."

His brow drew down. Now he knew he was getting close, but the music was drawing to an end, and she was pulling away in every sense.

He caught her by the hand when she went to walk away from him. "What does that mean, love?"

Her eyes flashed in a way he couldn't describe. "Nothing," she said. "It doesn't matter."

She walked away, but they were not done. He'd get to the bottom of his mysterious, unnerving, irritating ward if it killed him.

CHAPTER EIGHT

S HE NEVER SHOULD have opened her mouth.

Philippa couldn't shake Benedict's piercing glare for the next two hours. He followed her every move. And all from the sidelines. First with Hayden, and then with more friends as they joined their little circle. She'd been introduced to the Duke and Duchess of Raffian and then the Earl of Fallenmore and his fiancée, all of whom had been overly kind to her.

Just like everyone else here.

She didn't know what Lady Foster had told her friends before their arrival, but it was clear there'd been an agreement amongst these highborn ladies and gentlemen that she was a sympathetic charity case to be welcomed.

Well, a charity case with a fortune to her name.

The cooing voices, the kind inquiries… It was all so familiar. This was what her life in Italy had been like after her parents' passing. So much kindness and consideration it had nearly killed her.

And it was the same here. Except with Benedict. He was the only one who treated her like her own person. Not an orphan. Not *that poor girl*. Just her. For better or for worse.

"How are you settling in at Benedict's home?" Lady Raffian asked.

She was kind, the new duchess. Kind and young and surprisingly quiet. Not cold, but rather shy, Philippa suspected. She didn't seem to wish to be the center of attention, and it did not escape Philippa's notice that the duke hovered over his wife to protect her from the many curious party guests.

It was adorable, really, to see the powerful and arrogant duke fawning all over his own wife.

Philippa's benign answer to the duchess was cut short when Lady Raffian visibly stiffened. Philippa followed her gaze to see what the matter was and caught her staring at a rather insipid-looking gentleman. She'd met him briefly, but he left so little an impression she couldn't even remember his name.

Lady Raffian had been smiling but a moment ago, and her sudden sneer of disapproval seemed out of character. "I cannot imagine how Mr. Foley received an invitation," she murmured.

Benedict was at her side, and he murmured something low about how he would take care of it.

"Why?" Philippa asked. "What has he done?"

Benedict and Lady Raffian exchanged a quick look that made Philippa shift with displeasure. She did not enjoy being left out of secrets, but she most especially did not enjoy knowing that the gorgeous blonde before her shared a secret with Benedict.

"Nothing for you to worry about," Benedict said in a low voice, for her ears only.

"But—"

"Just steer clear of the man," he interrupted. "That's an order."

Philippa looked on in surprise as glances were exchanged, whispers passed about, and poor Mr. Foley was suddenly and noticeably snubbed. Those around him who'd been speaking to him turned away, and he went from one cluster to another, pretending to be indifferent as he was most clearly not welcomed into the bosom of society.

Lady Raffian turned to her with another smile. "My apologies, you were in the middle of speaking when I so rudely interrupted."

"Oh no, it's..." Philippa trailed off. She had questions, but mainly her stomach had soured.

That man, whoever he was, had clearly been cast out of high society's goodwill, for whatever petty reason, and meanwhile, she was here, welcome and accepted and...

It was all so very wrong. Though not nearly so bad as watching Lord Foster's reception. He'd hardly seemed to notice the way he was being watched and judged, but she had.

She'd watched every flinch, taken note of every whisper. She'd noticed above all that his mother had abandoned him to this fate as soon as they'd arrived.

She fidgeted with her reticule as Benedict joined them and soon their little group of close-knit friends were exchanging stories and quips, ignoring all the hangers-on walking close by and clearly angling to join in on the fun.

Philippa smiled and tried to act the part of Lord Foster's grateful ward.

Because she was grateful, of course.

But that did not change things. Now that the idea had taken hold, she'd become convinced that eschewing society was the only way forward for her. It wasn't what her parents would have wanted, but she'd disappointed them long ago.

And besides, they were dead.

What mattered now was living.

Which was why, when she and Benedict were once more alone in a carriage headed home, she made sure to make herself clear. The opportunity came when he asked her about her evening.

"It was fine, I suppose. Though I'm afraid it was all in vain."

"In vain?" He was eyeing her closely. He had been all night.

She smiled. "I shall not be marrying, Benedict."

His brows arched slightly. He'd been known to call her Philippa and even endearments, but she'd never outright called him by his given name before. It tasted delicious on her tongue. And the way he looked at her made that space between her thighs ache.

He didn't protest the intimacy of her calling him by his given name. A point she took to be in her favor. Instead, he leaned back in his seat with a lazy, heavy-lidded glower. "And why will you not be marrying, Philippa?"

She liked the fact he did not instantly argue. Perhaps she was making progress.

"I do not wish to be a lady of society."

He leaned back further, and she felt a shiver race through her at the heat in his eyes as he studied her. Her breathing grew labored as his dark gaze grew heavy and thoughtful. She was certain she could feel his eyes on her, hot and all-seeing.

"You seemed to enjoy yourself this evening," he said at last.

She jerked back in her seat, the words a splash of cold water. He couldn't have meant to hurt her, but he'd done it. "I…I…"

"When we were dancing," he continued.

He couldn't possibly mean it as an accusation, but it felt like one. Panic clawed at her.

His head tilted to the side and his eyes narrowed in scrutiny. "There were moments this evening when it truly seemed as though you were enjoying your first excursion in London society." A smile tugged at his lips. "Particularly when you were dancing."

Her lungs hitched.

Precisely. That was the problem right there. Dancing had been a transcendent experience. For long moments when he'd spun her in his arm, she'd forgotten her past. She'd always loved dancing, but it had been more than a year since she'd had the chance. She'd let herself be swept away by the music and the feel of his arms around her and had forgotten entirely that she didn't deserve to be enjoying herself. That she shouldn't be having fun.

"You seemed to be having a pleasant time making conversation with Lady Raffian and the others, as well," he continued. As if he were intent on pointing out her enjoyment.

She shifted in her seat. It was true. She and Lady Raffian had found a number of things to laugh about and discuss. The blonde beauty had been easy to like, despite that one cruel turn toward poor Mr. Foley. Whatever he'd done, he was clearly paying for it.

But aside from that, Lady Raffian and Benedict's friends had been diverting. Too diverting. She'd found herself laughing far too often. More nights like tonight—being accepted, distracted, surrounded by kindness, and her past forgotten...

It would become all too easy to forget herself. It would be much too simple to let herself be swept away by it all, to be the person they all thought her to be.

"I'm telling you, I will not marry," she said at last, her voice harder this time.

He arched a brow. "You seem awfully certain. What if your guardian arranges a marriage?"

She smirked. "I already told you I'd ruin it."

"I do believe you would, you naughty girl," he chided softly.

The low rumble of his voice in this enclosed space made her belly flutter, and she had to press her thighs together to fight a throbbing ache.

Then he looked away, out the window and into the night. "We'll talk about this tomorrow. It's too late to argue."

She wet her lips. The closer they got to his home, the more unsettled she felt. Memories of the night were mocking her.

She'd had fun, blast it all. She'd enjoyed herself. She'd acted the part of the sweet, innocent young victim, and it had felt...

Oh drat. It had felt good.

It was cowardly though. It was wrong, and deep inside her, she knew it.

His eyes widened when she slipped off her seat and onto his, so they were side by side.

"Philippa..." His tone was wary.

"Shh." She pressed a hand to his chest as she leaned in close, devouring his scent. So very masculine with a mix of soap and leather and spirits. His skin was hot to the touch when her nose grazed his neck. "Just let me pleasure you. That's all I ask."

His groan was satisfaction itself. He gripped her hand on his chest to hold it still. "I don't know why you're doing this, Philippa. I don't understand what you think you'll gain by being my mistress rather than marrying a suitable gentleman the way you ought."

She shook her head. "I told you I don't want all that…" She nodded in the direction they'd come. "I don't want society life."

"If that's true, then I can find you a place to live in the country," he said. "You can reside with my mother or with a paid companion."

There was a hint of desperation to his voice.

Forgotten in the countryside. With all the time in the world on her hands to relive the past. A fitting punishment, perhaps. But also…more than she could bear.

"That's not what I want," she whispered, her lips brushing his ear.

"And what is it that you want?" he asked.

To be ruined. To be destroyed. To be cast out.

The words hovered on her tongue. She settled for another truth. "To drown."

He turned his head to look at her, and she stole a kiss.

He didn't kiss her back, stilling instead. But she heard his breathing grow ragged as she moved her lips over his. After a few seconds, she pulled back to gauge his reaction.

His eyes were pitch black in the shadows, but she felt his stare burning her skin. "You'd make me even more of a monster so you might forget your pain?"

Her heart gave a jolt of alarm at that. Was that what he thought she was doing?

"No," she said too quickly. "I'd willingly, happily give you what you want, and in return, I'd receive…"

Pleasure.

Pain.

Escape.

She shook her head. "I'd get what I want, too."

His grip was tight on her hand that still clutched his chest, and he dragged it down until she touched his hard shaft.

They both gasped at the contact.

"You have no idea what I want," he growled.

He meant to frighten her away, but it would not work.

"I think I do," she whispered. "Remember, I am no innocent virgin."

"And I am no proper gentleman."

"Says the earl," she shot back with a smirk.

"Says the man responsible for killing his father and brother. The men who should have held the title."

She stopped breathing. His gaze held hers and she saw it. An echo of the pain she felt.

He understood guilt and regret.

She leaned forward with renewed vigor. "I can bring you pleasure, Benedict. I can help you forget."

We can help each other forget.

His gaze flickered over her face. "You know there are expectations when it comes to who I marry."

She nodded quickly. "I told you, I do not want marriage. I want to please you. I want pleasure and I want pain—" She leaned in and nipped his ear, making him hiss. "I want…I want…"

She stumbled to put it into words. For a moment, his gaze softened. "You want to feel."

"Yes." She hissed the word, because…*yes.* He understood. She couldn't bear these emotions any longer. She didn't want them on the inside. She needed to put it into physical form.

"I deserve to be punished," she admitted in a whisper. It was the closest she'd come to telling anyone the whole truth.

"I *want* to be punished." The thought of him taking her over his knee…of him growling out harsh, crude commands, ordering her about to satisfy his needs… That was what she wanted. What she craved above all. Her imagination alone had the heat inside of her intensifying, and she bit her lip to stifle a whimper as her sex dripped with her juices. "Punish me, my lord."

He growled. "You don't deserve punishment. You just need to be taken in hand."

She gulped as she pictured it. The way his large, scarred hand had locked on her breast. The way he would cover her, his weight crushing her...

With his free hand, he caught her chin and forced her to look at him.

She felt him harden further under her palm.

"You need someone to teach you a lesson."

She could see him losing the battle with his willpower. The heat in his eyes rivaled her own. Was he imagining it, too? Was he thinking of all the ways he would command her in the bedroom?

"A lesson?" she whispered.

His tongue flicked out and licked her lips, making her moan.

"You need to be taught how to get out of that head of yours," he continued. "How to leave the past in the past."

"Like you have done?" she whispered.

His smile was wry, and he didn't try and deny it. He understood her because he was there where she was. Trapped in the past.

His gaze was fixed on hers, but his voice grew distant. "Maybe we both need to learn our lesson."

She leaned into him, squeezing him hard. "Then teach me, my lord. Take me to your bed and teach me."

For a second, he wavered. She had him; she could feel it.

Satisfaction was just beginning to bloom when he pulled away from her, leaving her cold. "We'd only drag each other down."

The words stung, and she blinked rapidly as if waking from a dream.

They couldn't be right.

The carriage came to a stop, and he helped her out. She kept her head tipped down, so he would not see the tears in her eyes.

She was cold. Cold and empty all the way through. This guilt and grief and shame and self-hate had eaten away at her insides, leaving her hollow.

And after tonight it had become painfully clear. He was the only one who could fill that void. The understanding in his eyes, the way he saw it. Saw her. The way he knew when no one else comprehended just how wicked she was beneath the surface. Add to that his large frame, his overpowering body, his stern voice, and even his beastly scars, and he was the one who could drive it from her. He was the one who could make her feel again.

And as she headed to her bed that night, she vowed she'd do whatever it took to push him to the brink. To make him snap.

She needed his hands on her, and she'd have it tonight.

CHAPTER NINE

F OR THE SECOND time, Benedict woke to screams.

His feet hit the floor before his mind fully woke. He threw open Philippa's bedroom door seconds later and froze at the sight before him.

Candles were lit on either side of the bed, and…she wasn't screaming.

Philippa was moaning.

Her head thrown back, she moaned softer now as her hand slid between her thighs.

The air rushed from his lungs as he watched, paralyzed by the surge of heat that had made him hard with longing.

Her nightdress was hitched up to her waist, her long, slender legs parted slightly—just enough for him to see the dark thatch of curls between her thighs.

"What in the bloody hell are you doing?" he growled.

She lifted her head, her lips parted and wet, her eyes glimmering in the dark. "I need you, Benedict."

His mind went blank as heat seared his flesh and settled in his loins. His mind sputtered and halted to a stop.

What she was doing was wrong. So very wrong.

And it was the most erotic sight he'd ever seen.

She wriggled her hips, tossing her head. The room smelled of her sex, and the scent was nearly his undoing.

He told himself to walk away. To close the door and turn back.

But when she rubbed her fingers over her mound, her eyes fluttering shut—he found himself walking toward her again.

"I ache," she whimpered. Her eyelids cracked open enough for her to look straight at him, and there was genuine neediness there, a pleading. "Make me feel better?"

Bloody hell, she was temptation itself. His gaze fixed on her slender hand that was restlessly moving between her legs. For all her talk of experience, her efforts were clumsy and untutored. Restless to the point of desperation.

"Come for me," he commanded.

He shocked them both with that growl.

What was he doing? Some distant part of his brain revolted.

He was helping her find pleasure. That was all. Then he'd end this madness.

"H-how?" she asked.

His mouth watered as he imagined how he might show her. He'd part her thighs and bury his face in her wet heat until she screamed the house down. Luckily for everyone, his mother was a heavy sleeper and on a separate floor.

Not that he'd give into temptation. No, he'd just help her, that was all. And then he would leave.

"Slip your fingers between the folds of your sex," he said instead.

Her eyes widened slightly, and her naivete was on full display for one dazzling moment.

Who had taken her innocence but failed to show her how to find pleasure?

He'd murder the knave if he had a name.

"Like this?" She did as she was told, her middle finger sinking into her wet heat, and her hips coming up with a jerk. "Oh!"

A smile tugged at his lips at her shock. "I thought you said you'd been ruined."

"I have," she said quickly. "I just...I did not do this. Now what?"

He fought another grin at her impatient demand. Greedy girl. His cock was demanding attention, and he slid a hand over the straining bulge of his breeches as her gaze followed.

She was too tempting. He was struggling to remember all the reasons he couldn't take what she was offering.

Because you're not a monster, and the girl needs to wed.

But it wouldn't be so very wrong if he wed her, now would it?

The thought took hold and wouldn't let go.

She wet her lips, and for a moment, he was speechless at this spectacular sight. He stroked himself once, then forced himself to stop. Her breasts were straining against the fabric, the dark of her nipples visible through the thin cotton. Her quim was visibly wet, and her hand was shaking.

She needed someone to take over. Someone to show her what to do.

"Dip your finger down," he said, his voice little more than a rumble. "Find that tight little hole that needs to be filled."

"Like this?" she breathed. Her head tossed to the side as she touched her channel. A whimper escaped.

"Now slide your finger in," he said.

"I can't, it's so…so tight."

He nearly exploded right then and there. He had to clench his jaw and focus on his breathing. So tight. So wet.

Oh yes, he could only imagine.

"Let me see your fingers." What was he doing? He'd lost his mind.

But what was even more mad… She complied. Withdrawing her hand, her fingers trembled as she held them up to see how they glistened with her juices.

With a groan, his restraint snapped, and without thinking, he snagged her hand and thrust her fingers in his mouth. He needed to taste her.

Her eyes flew open in shock, her jaw gaping open as he

sucked off the sweet cream of her cunny. Her lips worked, but nothing came out.

He held her gaze and brought her hand down to cover his hard length. Her expression grew pained with need as she moaned again.

"Was this what you needed, love? Is that what you called out for?"

She nodded quickly.

"You're a naughty little tease, aren't you?"

"Yes, my lord," she whispered.

She was using that voice, the subservient little miss with her master.

He loved that tone. And he suspected she did, too. It was a role she played, but there was a truth to it. A need she couldn't put into words any other way.

He understood it—at least part of the mystery that was his tempting ward. She was floundering in her dark, bottomless emotions and desperate for someone else to take control. To tell her what to do and how to be.

Someone to save her.

The realization struck in a heartbeat, and it rattled him to his core. Her hand was still on his cock, but this new understanding touched something far deeper inside of him.

His heart twisted with an overwhelming surge of protectiveness and affection.

Tenderness the likes of which he'd never known made his insides quake and when it was all said and done, he had the distinct and terrifying sensation that nothing would ever be the same.

He would never be the same.

"Will you take me?" She slid her legs further apart in a silent offer that made him groan. "Will you show me what you like?"

He knew his answer, just like he knew what it meant. It changed everything. The future was suddenly laid out before him, irreversible and undeniable.

It all felt so inevitable. Maybe there'd never been any other path for him or for her.

But he had to give her one last chance to run. He had to try, at least, for her sake.

He dropped her hand and sank onto the bed beside her, trying not to notice the way her breathing had turned to short, choppy bursts.

The girl was desperate for relief. And he could give her that. But not until she understood what this meant.

"You want me to fuck you, love?" he asked. "You want me to use that sweet body of yours and ride that tight little quim?"

His voice was gruff, and the hand that cupped one of her breasts and pinched her nipple was anything but gentle. Part of him hoped he'd scare her off, while another part of him was begging for this to be real. That she could truly be his.

Her back arched with a whimper as if she was trying to get even closer to his hand, her body asking for more. "Yes," she hissed. "Please, my lord. Please, please, please—"

He crushed his lips to hers to squelch her begging. It was too heady, too intoxicating to hear her plead for his touch. Him. The scarred, broken beast.

He didn't deserve her. That much was certain. But she wanted him, and he could protect her. He could help her.

And when she was healed and realized she was stuck with him forever?

He flinched at the thought and pulled back. Her lips were already slightly swollen and wet from that bruising kiss.

"I need you," she whispered. And there was no artifice in her tone. No acting and no teasing taunts.

His heart had been stolen, that much was clear as he gazed down at her wide eyes and long hair splayed out around her just like in his fantasies.

His heart belonged to her now, but she couldn't know that.

He swallowed hard, shutting out her pleading gaze and the way she writhed and wiggled beneath his touch.

He'd give her one last chance to reconsider her actions before he damned her to his hell. "You sure you want this, love? Think hard because there's no turning back."

She nodded eagerly, but he cupped her chin in his hand to hold her face still, to force her gaze to meet his. Her lips parted with a gasp, and her gaze grew distant and dreamy at the rough handling.

Oh yes, his wild little hellion wanted to be tamed, that much was clear.

"Look at me," he commanded.

Her gaze focused on his eyes.

"Tell me you know what it means if I take you tonight."

She blinked once, twice. He could see her mind trying to work. "I understand."

"Say it."

Her tongue flicked out to wet her lips, and he groaned softly at the sight. "It means...it means I'm ruined." Her gaze was so soft and sweet, it nearly broke him in two. "I understand the consequences of my actions, Benedict. I know what this means."

He stared at her speechless for a second because...he was a monster. He was not kind, nor was he a true gentleman. That much had been widely known even before he'd gotten his father and brother killed. But did she really think him so unfeeling that he would ruin her?

He leaned down closer. "Wrong answer, love."

"Then what does it mean?" she whispered.

"If I take you now, you're mine." His voice was as hard as his erection at the thought. *Mine, mine, mine.* The word thrummed through him and pushed aside the last of his reason. "If we do this now, you are mine forever. Understand?"

CHAPTER TEN

*M*INE FOREVER.

Her breath rushed from her.

She knew what he was doing. Did he have any idea that those words made the longing inside her intensify a hundred times over? All it would take was one touch of his hand between her thighs for him to know just how much his words moved her.

He released her chin from his merciless grip and shifted to put one hand on either side of her, caging her beneath his scarred, muscled chest.

"If we do this," he continued in a low rumble. "You will be mine to do whatever I want with. Mine to use. Mine to pleasure. Mine to discipline."

He was trying to frighten her. A last-ditch effort. She could see it all so clearly, just like she could see *him* in the candlelight. He'd moved into the flickering glow, and she could see in stark clarity the two sides of this man. The scarred half was undeniably ugly. The way it twisted his mouth and pulled at his features made him look the beast that he clearly thought himself to be.

She reached a hand up to cup the scarred cheek, so at odds with the right side of his face, which was everything noble and handsome.

He tensed beneath her touch but did not pull away. He let her touch him, and her heart seemed to trip in its racing.

"You'll be mine," he said again. A growl. A rumble she could feel low in her belly.

A promise that felt like the most binding vow.

His to command and his to discipline…

A lightness stole into her chest at his words. She wasn't frightened. She wasn't sure he could ever frighten her. She'd seen too much of him beyond the scars and the temper. Instead, she felt something knotted and heavy uncoil within her at those possessive words, the threats, and the commands. Something eased and relaxed, a weight taken off her that she hadn't been able to see or put into words.

"Yes," she said with a nod, her gaze colliding with his. "I'm yours."

A flare of surprise lit his eyes, there and gone. For a second, there was tension between them. He was stiller than ever before as he hovered over her.

But then, like a wall crashing to the ground, his restraint gave way. He crushed his mouth to hers, capturing her lips in a bruising, ruthless kiss that made her moan and arch up to meet him.

This. Yes, this was what she wanted. To lose herself. To be swept away.

And not with gentle touches and sweet words, but with punishing kisses and rough, firm hands. Satisfaction exploded in her chest when he settled his weight over the top of her. Hot and heavy, his chest had no softness about it, only the rough scrape of his scars. One of his thick, hair-covered thighs settled between hers, and she let out a sharp exhale at the friction and heat between her legs.

She found her hips moving restlessly against his thigh as his tongue slid between her lips, invading her mouth. Claiming her lips.

That was what this was. A claiming. He was taking what she'd been teasing him with these past weeks. He was taking ownership, and for the first time in a year, her mind was blissfully blank beneath this onslaught of her senses.

The heavy cloak of guilt and shame was replaced by the hard weight of him, the incessant demands of his mouth, his hands, his lower half, which was grinding against her as she wriggled her hips for more.

His breeches were between them still, but she could feel his hard shaft prodding against her sex. When it rubbed against that hard nub he'd led her to explore, she whimpered into his mouth.

He growled in response, slanting his mouth over hers as if he could devour her neediness. The stubble of his jaw was rough against her face, a scarred, calloused palm scraped against her skin as he cupped her neck and squeezed before grabbing the neckline of her nightdress and, in one quick jerk, tore it down the middle.

He leaned back to see all that he'd exposed. Resting back on his haunches, her sex throbbed in agony at the loss of that hard heat and the tantalizing friction. Now she was cold, and the loss of his weight had thoughts flooding back into her brain.

Wicked, unholy girl.

She tossed her head from side to side and reached for him, pressing her palms to his searingly hot abdomen. He growled at the touch and reached for the tattered edges of the torn fabric, making short work of ripping it the rest of the way, so she was spread bare beneath him.

Your dark soul belongs in hell. You'll ruin yourself and destroy this family.

She squeezed her eyes shut as if that could wipe away her father's voice. But the feel of Benedict's large, rough hand clamping around her jaw had her eyes flying open.

"Eyes on me," he said.

She swallowed hard, some part of her latching onto that commanding growl like it was a rope leading to her salvation. He held her head still as his gaze devoured her from head to toe.

She fought the urge to fidget with nerves and embarrassment.

No one had ever seen her like this, naked and vulnerable. But she did as he'd commanded and kept her eyes open. And when he glanced back up and his gaze met hers, she felt a satisfaction in obeying him.

"Good girl," he murmured as he slid himself over her again, surprisingly graceful for such a large, muscled body.

His hand released her chin as he caged her beneath him. "Are you frightened?"

She shook her head quickly. "No."

She knew what he meant. The way she'd squeezed her eyes shut before when he'd handled her body without tenderness.

Not harsh, though. Not cruel.

She shook her head again, her voice stronger. "No, I'm not scared of you."

I'm scared of me. Of the monster I am inside.

His eyes held hers for a moment before he nodded. She thought maybe he'd even read her thoughts. He lowered his head, but rather than kiss her, his lips found the sensitive skin beneath her ear, and he nuzzled her there, his hot breath making her shiver and pant.

He slid a palm over her left breast, pausing to tweak the nipple so hard it made her hips arch up with her gasp. She tried to keep him there, her hands gripping his hot, hard back muscles as she pressed her breast up for more, but he was sliding that rough palm over her belly and lower, lower...

She cried out when he found her heat.

Lustful, wanton little creature.

She pressed her face into the crook of his neck and his groan next to her ear made her shiver. His fingers were merciless and firm in their exploration of that wet heat between her folds. His thick fingers slid with sure strokes, flicking over that hard, sensitive nub and then lower, stopping to tease the edges of her channel, probing a little before sliding back up to rub that hard nub.

Her hips jerked beneath him as she clung to his shoulders. Her body was out of her control. It was his to command now, and she grinned at the thought as she opened her mouth to taste the salt on his skin.

A little lick of her tongue had him stilling, his breath hot and sharp against her ear.

She tried it again, this time nipping at the hot skin beneath her mouth until he groaned and pulled his head back to kiss her with such crushing force, it stole her breath.

When he began to push one finger inside her, she tensed at the intrusion, which was at once so good and so odd.

"So tight." He must have felt her or heard her breath growing choppy as his finger probed deeper inside her, thick and demanding. "I don't want to hurt you, love."

"You won't," she panted. "You can't, remember? I am no innocent."

You're nothing more than a dirty little whore.

She bit him again, harder this time, and with a growl, he went back to devouring her mouth with a kiss that brooked no arguments. He removed his hand to unbutton his breeches and push them down, but all she knew was that she was cold and bereft except for the feel of his lips on hers.

She clung to that sensation, her fingers sliding into his hair to hold him closer. When her palm touched the left, scarred side of his face, he stilled for a second.

She waited to see if he'd pull away or shove her hand aside, but with a shudder he relented, letting her touch him like he was touching her. As one hand shoved down his breeches, the other was greedily groping her breasts, as if he couldn't get enough of the feel of her flesh in his palm. Kneading and tugging on her nipples, he settled his weight beside her.

"Take me," she whimpered when he pulled back. "Make me yours."

"Spread your legs," he commanded, his breath hot against her lips.

There was something crude about the demand, and that made her sex throb painfully as she followed his orders, spreading her thighs wide and biting her lip as he pulled back to view her.

She looked down, too, and spread wide as she was, she barely recognized herself in the moonlight. She truly was the wanton slattern her father thought her to be. Her sex was swollen and wet, the dark thatch of curls no longer hiding her from view.

"So wet," he muttered. His large, calloused thumb swept over her nub at the apex of her folds, making her cry out at the sharp jolt of pleasure.

His lips tugged up in response, and his gaze was frighteningly hungry as he took in the bare breasts, the flat belly, and that wet, secret place between her thighs.

He wet his lips, and the only sound in the room was their panting breath. She looked lower. She'd never seen his manhood, and she wanted to see it. "Can I...May I..."

Her voice was softer than she'd ever heard it, and she shifted to reach for him. He pulled away out of reach, but his low chuckle warmed her and sent a trickle of new heat through her limbs.

"You want this, love?" He held himself in his hand, and she tried not to let her shock show.

She failed if his next chuckle was anything to go by.

"Soon I'm going to have you touch me just like this." He stroked the length in his hand, and she watched with wide eyes as it swelled even further.

Her mouth went dry with nerves as her sex grew even wetter than before.

His gaze held hers with a dark promise. "Next time you talk back to me like a little brat, I'm going to have you suck this until you've learned how to be a good girl, hmm?"

Heat speared her from the inside out, making her inner muscles clench and her back arch. "Yes," she hissed.

That was exactly what she wanted. How did he know? She could picture it so clearly it hurt. His hands were rough in her hair as he slid that thick shaft between her lips with his gruff voice and coarse commands.

Her hips came off the bed. "Please, my lord. Let me taste

you."

His growl was a low rumble. "My naughty girl."

She moaned with desire. Those words were so wrong, but on his lips, they sounded like an endearment. They were a balm, an encouragement.

Yes, she was naughty. Wicked. Maybe even evil.

And he wanted her for it.

"You want this inside you, pet?" he asked as he stroked himself harder and faster, his voice a taunt and a tease. He leaned down and kissed her lower belly, making her muscles clench and flutter.

"Yes," she whispered, ignoring the bit of fear that the sight of his erection had caused.

He was big. So very big. And he seemed to be getting ever bigger with each stroke. Her inner thigh muscles made as if to clamp shut when he shifted, but she fought the urge to protect herself.

She reached down again, her fingers itching to touch him, to stroke him like he was doing. But more than that, her sex was throbbing for relief, her nipples were too tight and hard, and they were aching to be crushed against his chest again, to rub against the wiry hair there.

She thrust her hips up like the wild wanton she was. "Make me yours," she said again. This time she begged. She had no pride left, only need.

Make me forget. Make me powerless. Make me beg and cry and—

She gasped when his hard shaft found her entrance. She bit her lip when he nudged the tip inside of her as his weight came over the top of her.

And despite her best efforts, she let out a scream of pain when he thrust himself inside of her.

CHAPTER ELEVEN

B ENEDICT FROZE.

It was the most difficult thing he'd ever done, but he tensed his muscles and stilled as a rush of cold shock hit him straight between the eyes.

"You're…" His face was still next to her head, and he pulled back to see her eyes.

Her pained, shocked, horrified eyes.

"You're a *virgin*," he bit out.

She squeezed her eyes shut. There was no denying it. He might not have taken a virgin before, but there was no confusion over the barrier he'd just broken through.

Brutally and in one hard thrust.

"Christ," he muttered through clenched teeth.

Her chest rose and fell quickly beneath him, and a bead of sweat trailed down her temple as she grimaced in pain.

He started to ease back, guilt and shame making his heart pound, but he stopped when her fingers dug into his back. "Don't," she whispered.

Horror flooded his veins as the reality of what he'd just done set in.

Horror…and fury. Fury, too. She'd told him she wasn't innocent, for God's sake. She'd told him she'd had a lover. She'd thrown her experience in his face on multiple occasions.

He glared down at her now. Clearly, she'd lied.

The muscles around her mouth pinched, and her nostrils flared as she drew in a deep breath. His anger sputtered and extinguished at the sight of her pain.

He kissed her forehead and then the tip of her nose. She let out a shaky breath, her grip loosening slightly on his shoulders.

"Let me pull out, love," he said. "It's too much for you."

Her eyes snapped open, and he found himself staring directly into her clear eyes, which looked dark and endlessly deep in the shadows. "No," she said again. Lifting her legs, she wrapped them around him until her heels dug into his arse, and he was so deep inside her, he nearly lost control.

He grit his teeth and focused on the way her eyes glittered with emotion in the moonlight. Emotions too complicated to name, but identifiable all the same.

He knew them well, this motley mix of desire and fear, shame and hope. Staring into her eyes was heady. Intoxicating. Like looking into a gypsy's tea leaves and seeing his past and his future all at once.

"I need this," she whispered. Her hips arched up. "Please."

Tension knotted in his back and made his jaw hard as stone.

Her voice was husky with desire and laced with pain. "I need *you.*"

That did it. He buried himself deeper without thinking, sheer animal instinct taking over before he could stop himself.

Her head fell back with her satisfied grunt.

"I'm hurting you," he said through a clenched jaw.

"I don't care." Her whisper turned to a moan when he circled his hips slightly.

He studied her features, still tight with discomfort, but there was desire there, too. Her eyelids were heavy, her gaze growing more distant and dazed with each labored breath.

He'd told himself he wouldn't touch her anymore, but he couldn't stop himself from dropping a kiss to her collarbone.

She arched up, thrusting her lovely tits so close to his mouth he couldn't resist the invitation. He lapped at one nipple until it was a hard pebble beneath his tongue, and she was wriggling her hips for more contact. Then he sucked that stiff peak into his mouth, sucking gently at first, and then harder when she cried out and buried her hands in his hair to hold him close.

He growled as pleasure shot down his spine and settled in his loins, his bollocks tightening with anguish and the need for release. But he kept his bottom half still, focusing all of his attention on her perfect breasts. He tried his best to ignore the sweet painful squeeze of her tight channel, but Christ she was tighter than he could have ever imagined. She was tight...and wet. For him.

The thought was humbling. He'd do whatever it took to bring back that pleasure she'd found before with his touch.

With one hand, he kneaded the soft flesh of one luscious breast while his mouth worked the other, alternating sides as her breathing became pants and her moans turned to whimpers.

"Please, please, please," she was chanting by the time he lifted his head.

He rewarded her with a kiss that startled him with its intimacy.

He'd kissed countless women before, though very few ladies. He'd even kissed women he'd liked before, including Francesca, whom he'd fancied himself in love with before she'd shown her true nature. But no kiss had ever felt like this.

This was...different.

Unsettlingly so. He'd never seen Philippa so vulnerable, and a surge of protectiveness had him kissing her gingerly, trying to tell her something he didn't know how to put into words. Her lips clung to his, her tongue warm and sweet as she tasted him with soft touches and gentle licks.

It was...tender.

But all at once, she tore her lips away with a shake of her head. "No more kissing."

He stared at her in surprise, but in a heartbeat, he realized she must have been turned off by the feel of his scarred skin against her flawless cheeks.

He swallowed down a wave of disgust with himself for forgetting for a moment who he was now. Who he'd become.

He'd become a beast who stole a young lady's virginity.

She gripped his head between her hands, forcing his gaze to meet hers.

"I need you to take me," she said. There was desperation there she didn't try to hide. "I need you to take me, rough and hard."

The words worked a spell on him and made his already tight bollocks tighten even further. He groaned. "I don't want to hurt you, love."

She exhaled sharply. "I want it. I need it. Please, my lord." Her gaze was pleading. "Please."

He finally gave in to the need that made his hard member feel like it might shatter from being so rigid, but it was with small, gentle thrusts that required every bit of his self-control.

"Yes," she whispered against his lips. "More. Harder."

He shook his head. "I'll hurt you."

Her expression shifted so suddenly it startled him anew. She bared her teeth in a grimace as she pressed her heels down and slammed her tight quim up. "Don't you understand, I want you to. I deserve it. Pound into me and make me scream."

A chill shot through him, cold enough to break through his lust. This was it. He was getting to the heart of her, and what he saw shook him. "Why?" he demanded, giving her one hard thrust as she asked. "Tell me why."

Her breath hitched, and her eyes rolled back with a moan of pleasure. "More."

"Tell me why you deserve it first," he murmured against her lips, rolling his hips to tease that spot inside of her that made her whimper.

"Because..." She used her thighs, her feet, and her hands to try and urge him on as she bucked wildly beneath him.

"Because why?" he demanded. He caught her by the chin and kissed her hard. "Tell. Me. Why."

"Because I deserve it," she blurted. "Because I am wicked and evil and cruel and mean."

Each word struck his skin like the lash of a whip. Not just the words themselves, but the self-hatred in her voice, the agony in her eyes. He couldn't take it. Seeing that in her. He'd seen it enough in the mirror, but to see it in her innocent, sweet eyes...

He would not stand for it.

Using his grip on her chin he tried to get her to meet his stare, but her gaze was distant and filled with pain. "Listen to me, love."

When she tried to look away, he dropped his hand to her slim, soft, tender throat and squeezed just tightly enough to shock her into the present. Her gaze collided with his—totally open and unguarded for the first time since they'd met.

"There will be some pain," he said. "I cannot help that. But there will be more pleasure, and you will take it."

She opened her mouth as if to protest, and he drew his hips back and rammed into her, making her cry out instead.

"I'm going to fill you up and fuck you hard. And you, my love...you are going to ride my cock until you find pleasure, do you hear me?"

She started to shake her head from side to side, but her hips were eagerly rising for more.

"You are mine, remember?" he growled against her ear.

She stopped shaking her head, and he could have sworn he saw relief in her eyes when she gazed back at him. "Yes, yes, I'm yours."

"Which means you will do as I say," he said as he rocked his hips, drawing his hard shaft in and out of her wet, tight cunny with agonizingly slow thrusts.

"Yes," she whispered.

He nipped at her bottom lip. "Good girl."

"I'm not a good girl," she said, a hint of that sadness still there.

"You are for me, aren't you?"

She hesitated for only a second, but when he thrust into her hard, his member filling her deep, she cried out with a *yes* that brought him to the edge of climax.

"That means you obey my order," he continued. It didn't escape his notice the way she responded physically to his commands. Her inner muscles tightened when he gave her commands, even as the rest of her seemed to melt into the bed, supple and pliant as a cat begging to be stroked.

He sucked on a nipple as his hands stroked her sides, her neck, her arms.

"I'll obey," she whimpered in his ear.

"Good girl," he said again, feeling her shiver in response. "Then listen closely, love." He pulled back to meet her gaze. "You will take me inside you, and you will chase the pleasure until you explode."

Confusion clouded her eyes. "Explode?"

His lips twitched up at his saucy little wench's naivete. "You'll see," he grunted. "Don't you dare fight it. Don't you dare deny yourself pleasure."

Her eyes glinted with a familiar mischief. "Or what?"

He pinched her nipple hard until she gasped, her channel tightening so fiercely he almost came right then and there.

Then she smiled up at him, a satisfied little kitten. "You know that only makes me want to get in trouble, don't you?"

He choked on a huff of amusement that startled him. He'd never once had the desire to laugh during sex before. He rocked into her, and she lifted her hips to meet him. He dropped a light kiss on the corner of her mouth. "You know that only makes me hope that you disobey, don't you?"

He felt her smile against his cheek as she giggled softly. "Sounds like we're both in for trouble."

He growled his agreement, but soon enough neither could speak because the pace of his thrusts was growing harder and faster. He reached between them to stroke her slick heat, rubbing and flicking the tight sensitive pearl, making her eyes flare wide with shock before she cried out, her legs clenching around him and her fingernails digging into his back as her inner muscles milked him over and over.

He groaned and buried his face against the heat of her neck as he pumped into her hard and fast until his own release barreled into him and sent him flying as he filled her with his seed.

He couldn't move for a long moment as he rested his head against her breast, listening to her heart pounding.

When he could, he shifted, slowly pulling out of her to rest his weight at her side, his hand settling over her belly. He was so much bigger than her, and he was overwhelmed by that wave of tender protectiveness, again, as his fingers lightly stroked her silky skin.

His seed was in there. He'd known from the moment he'd decided to take what she was offering what this would mean. But now he faced that decision with new stark clarity that probably should have been terrifying…but wasn't.

If anything, it merely felt…inevitable.

He thought she might have fallen asleep when he started to roll away from her, but her sleepy voice mumbled, "Where are you going?"

He didn't answer, finding his way to her washbasin in the dark and wetting a cloth. When he came back to the bed, he found she'd rolled onto her belly, her hair strewn over her face and the pillow as her breathing grew deep and even.

Her brows drew down, and she gave a little jerk as the wet cloth moved over her thighs.

"Easy, love," he whispered when she tried to pull away from his ministrations. He continued his work with gentle movements, cleaning away the blood and his semen from her thighs and her sex.

"Stop being nice to me," she murmured, her voice muffled by the pillow where her face was still half-buried. "You're not supposed to be nice to me."

He stilled, his heart giving a harsh slam at those words. But he kept his voice even. "Why not?"

"Because you're just not."

Little brat. He eyed her bare bottom, his member already stirring at the image of the tupping to come if he were to give her a spanking for using that childish tone.

He could see it so clearly, the way she'd gasp and moan as her bottom turned red and the flesh of her arse jiggled beneath his palm. And when she was writhing with need, her sex swollen and dripping wet with desire, he'd lift that bottom up in the air, and he'd ram his cock into her from behind.

His breathing grew harsh as the image filled his mind. One day. Soon. He took a deep breath and glared at his half-erect member. But not now. She'd be too sore.

So instead, he settled his hand on the round curve of her bottom, and his fingers bit into her soft skin reflexively. Rather than squirm in protest, she arched her hips up for more. Even half-asleep, she responded to his touch.

Tomorrow maybe. Or the day after that. He shifted on the edge of the bed to ease the ache in his loins. There'd be plenty of time to take her every way he could imagine.

He'd make her come apart with a scream every morning, noon, and night. He'd lick her quim until she begged for mercy. He ran a hand over her smooth back as his imagination ran wild. He'd take her on the dining room table when she gave him that haughty little smirk and have her ride him until she screamed in ecstasy during a walk in the woods.

He'd fuck that pretty mouth of hers whenever she dared to say that she was evil.

His brow furrowed as he stared down at her, her bare back rising and falling with deep, even breaths. Her hair was strewn about, and with a light touch, he brushed a lock out of her face.

She looked just as innocent as she was in sleep. And for a long time, he sat there and watched her. Those lush lips slightly parted, her lashes long and dark against her pale cheek.

I am wicked and evil and cruel and mean.

He frowned down at her. That was what she truly believed. But why? Who'd told her such a thing?

She was naughty, yes. Willful and stubborn, no doubt. Lustful and passionate, definitely. But there was nothing evil about that. There was nothing wrong with her, though she seemed convinced that there was.

To him, she was... well, not perfect.

But then again, neither was he. But maybe that was the point. He wouldn't know what to do with a woman who was kind and gentle, through and through.

No, his Philippa was not a proper young lady, but she was perfect in her own odd way. She was complicated, and all the more appealing for her complexity. He let out a short huff of laughter as he considered her.

She certainly wasn't boring. If anything, she was a riddle.

There was a gentleness to her that tempered her brash behavior, a strength that belied her small stature, and a sweet innocence and vulnerability that she hid behind tempting smiles and saucy flirtation. Beyond that, she had passion the likes of which he'd never seen. Not even the most experienced mistress had brought him such pleasure in bed. She'd thrown herself into the act with wild impetuous abandon.

He smoothed a hand over her lower back. Was that why she thought herself evil? Because she had longings and desires that were considered inappropriate for a young lady?

He scowled at the thought. He supposed her issues went deeper than that, but that was a good enough place to start.

How to prove to her that there was nothing wrong with having needs? That to have a salacious, insatiable appetite in the bedroom was a good thing.

Or it would be...once they were married.

CHAPTER TWELVE

"M ARRIED?" PHILIPPA'S VOICE was a piercing scratch that sent the bird on the windowsill flying with a squawk.

Benedict went about his morning routine as if she hadn't just hurt both their ears. "That's what I said." He tossed her a dismissive look over his shoulder as he fastened his cufflinks. "What else did you expect?"

Her jaw hung open as she stared at him with wide eyes. What else, indeed?

Heat seared her cheeks as her sleep-addled brain pieced it together. "This is because I'm a virgin, isn't it?"

He turned again, this time to give her a ferocious scowl, but she wasn't afraid.

She clutched the covers to her bare chest. Well, she *was* afraid, but not of his scowls. Not even of him.

"Benedict, you are overreacting," she said.

This…was the wrong thing to say.

He forgot entirely about setting his clothing to rights and turned to her with a calm, steady gaze that was much more terrifying than his glares and glowers. For this steady gaze spoke of determination. Resolve. Whatever he'd decided, it was as good as done in his book.

Her brows drew together in a scowl of her own. *Insufferable man.*

"Yes," he drawled slowly as he stalked toward the edge of the bed. "Let's talk about the fact that, despite your claims, you were indeed an innocent."

Her chin came up even as her skin burned beneath his perusal. "Not an *innocent*."

At his arched brows, she added, "Just because I was not entirely ruined does not mean I'm innocent."

He stopped walking, pausing a few feet from the bed to stare at her in a way that left her feeling far more naked and vulnerable than she had the night before. He seemed to be staring straight through her, all the way inside her...

She wriggled beneath the blankets and cast a longing glance toward the door.

She'd missed her chance to escape, that much was clear. When she'd first woken to morning light streaming in through her windows, she'd discovered an empty place beside her in bed.

Smart, she'd thought. He'd slipped out before the servants could notice and—

Wrong. The moment she'd started to think it, he'd come striding in from the adjacent room, his hair wet and his scarred torso dripping with bathwater, a towel slung low around his hips.

For a moment there, she'd been unable to breathe thanks to the striking sight of him before her, so large and hard and so...so Benedict. He'd stopped to take her in as well, and for a moment, she'd gotten hot all over, convinced that he'd come right back into this bed to pick up where they'd left off.

The sore place between her thighs had ached at the thought, and she'd squeezed her legs together tight while offering him a small, inviting smile.

He'd turned away with a grunt and had headed over to her dressing area where a fresh set of clothes had been laid out for him, along with a tray of breakfast for two.

Her mouth had gone dry then, her vision cloudy as her brain tried to reconcile what was happening. Servants had been here, to draw a bath and bring the food and—

And perhaps he did not mind them knowing she was his mistress.

So yes, the fact that he hadn't tried to hide this interlude from the servants was her first hint that this was not going according to plan. But she still hadn't expected *this*.

As if he were discussing the weather, he'd reached for his shirt and tugged it on while saying, "I'll have the banns posted shortly, but you should prepare yourself for the fact that Mother will no doubt want to announce our marriage plans at tonight's soiree. She'll be worried about the servants talking, no doubt."

He'd gone off muttering about how his mother might not approve, but she'll make the best of it. And all the while, Philippa had sat there in shocked silence.

Until she hadn't.

"But…*marriage*?" she squeaked again, her voice still unfortunately high. She made an effort to drop it, to sound calm even as her belly fluttered with nerves. "Have you lost your mind?"

Again. Wrong thing to say.

He arched his brows, his voice dangerously calm. "You are doubting my sanity?" He moved closer until he was right beside her, and his fingers moved over her cheeks, clasping her jaw with a touch that was so gentle and so very at odds with the storm raging in his eyes. "I am not the one who lured you to my bed, love. And I'm not the one who lied about—"

"That *is* it," she cried, jerking her head away with an odd sense of triumph. "My virginity. If that's the only reason you think you have to marry me, then let me assure you—"

"Don't be daft," he snapped. "I'd planned to marry you from the start."

"From the…what?"

He glared down at her, and she felt every inch the recalcitrant child.

His fists came down on either side of her, making the mattress sink as he loomed over her. "You did not think I would fuck my ward and leave her to face ruin, did you?"

She cringed at the harsh word, even though she knew that was exactly what they'd done. This had not been some romantic interlude, merely lust.

But even as she thought it, her mind chose that moment to call up the heart-aching tenderness in his eyes when he'd realized she was hurting. The painfully gentle way he'd touched her and held her and took care of her after.

She tore her gaze away as a wave of emotions crashed over her.

"I knew I would marry you before I ever set hands on you," he said. "Your virginity did not change anything except for the fact that I may very well tan your hide for lying to me the way you did."

Her cheeks still burned as she stared down at her bent knees and her clasped hands. Shame slithered through her at what she'd done. But she hadn't meant to trap him into marriage. Quite the opposite.

"I don't need you to marry me," she said through a tight throat. "I don't wish for you to—"

"Too bad. You should have thought of that before you threw yourself at me," he snapped. "Now you're stuck with me. I suppose that's punishment enough, eh?"

Her head came up because, beneath his anger, she could have sworn she'd heard…hurt.

But that couldn't be right. She couldn't have hurt his feelings by wanting a physical relationship and nothing more.

Could she?

Confusion rattled her even further, and she glanced around her, desperate for some sort of escape from his all-seeing glare. All she found were the walls of this room. Her new home. She'd thought these quarters spacious and opulent only the night before, but now it was closing in on her. "You cannot marry me," she said, her fingers clutching the covers tight between her hands.

"Why not?"

She thought she caught a flicker of amusement there in his

gaze and definitely a hint of concern.

"Why *not?*" she repeated. Her voice was too shrill again, but there was nothing for it. Her insides were tied in knots she couldn't begin to unwind. She didn't even know where to begin. "Because you cannot," she ended lamely.

He eased away from her, making the bed dip as he sank onto the edge. His weight had her fighting to keep her balance, lest she topple into his arms.

And would that be the worst fate you could imagine?

Truly, it was tempting. Last night was the first time in more than a year that she'd felt some relief from the crushing guilt. It was the first time the ghost of her former life no longer haunted her.

But that had been last night. That had been in the darkness of the evening and under the heady influence of his kisses and his touch.

This was different.

This was the cold light of day, and it was their future at stake. *His* future.

"I am not meant to be a countess," she said, the words coming out on a rush of desperation.

His smirk was wry and bitter. "Nor was I meant to be an earl, but here I am."

"That's different."

"Is it?"

She shook her head with a frown. "It is, and you know it. You were born to this family—"

"And I ruined it single-handedly," he said. "I don't see how that makes me fit to be earl."

The way he said it—so plainspoken. So brutally honest without rationalizing or excuses. It terrified her. "You ruined it?" The question was small. "How?"

She'd heard the rumors, of course. Even in the ballroom, she'd caught wind of the gossip. That he was somehow to blame for the fire that claimed his father and brother. And he had openly claimed responsibility for his family's deaths. But she still did not know the story, and she couldn't deny her curiosity. She nibbled on her lip. "Is it true then? What they say?"

He dipped his chin, his eyes dark and grim.

"I'm sorry," she whispered.

And she was. Because she understood his pain better than he could know.

"I am, too," he said. "I should never have brought my mistress to our family home. I never should have gotten so far in my cups. I never should have fought with the woman who I'd already realized was mad." He shook his head wearily. "There are so many things I would change if I could go back."

She nodded, her throat too choked with emotion to speak. They sat in silence for a long moment as she thought about what he'd said. "She set the fire? Your mistress?"

Another short nod. "It appears that way. The fire started in my brother's room, and she was in there with him. Earlier that day while we were fighting and I was drunk, she'd screamed something about how if I didn't want her, she'd find another to take my place." He lifted a shoulder. "It was only later I realized she meant my brother."

"Do you think the fire was intentional?"

"Yes." He didn't even hesitate. "I know her, and I know my brother. When I first met her, I found her histrionics amusing, her melodramatic flair intriguing." He snorted. "I didn't see the truth of her madness for far too long. But my brother had. He was the smart one, you know." Another bitter smile. "He'd always known her for what she was, and he was furious with me for daring to bring her into our home when Mother and Father were in attendance."

She watched him for a long while, her heart in her throat as he spoke.

"But that was part of the reason I did it," he admitted. "I was always acting out. Always rebelling. In hindsight, I don't even know why."

Tears welled in her eyes. He might have been speaking on her behalf. He might as well have been in her head.

Why must you misbehave? Her mother's voice was clear as day in her mind, spoken only days before her death.

Because she's wicked, her father had answered when she'd failed to respond.

Their wicked, evil, amoral girl. That was who she'd always been.

That was who she was.

"My father died trying to save my brother." Benedict's voice brought her back to the present with a start.

"I'm sorry," she said. But even as she said it, she knew how useless it was. It was the trite, meaningless phrase everyone said to her, and here she was saying it now. Because, really, what else was there to say?

"Yes, well…" His voice was gruff, but the tone filled with new forced energy as he looked around them, clearly ready to change the topic. "I suppose I thought you ought to know the truth behind the rumors." His gaze came back to collide with hers. "Now that you are to be my wife."

She inhaled so quickly she nearly choked. For a second there, she'd forgotten what this argument was all about.

"You cannot be serious," she said.

His hard glare said otherwise.

"I'm not fit to—"

"We've been over all that," he said, sounding bored as he got to his feet to resume getting ready for the day. "Doesn't matter your connections, what matters is that you could even now be carrying my child."

She gaped down at her belly in horror. "No, I cannot…I mean, that isn't—"

"Philippa…" His look of utter discomfort had her going still. "You do understand where babies come from, don't you?"

She rolled her eyes. "Of course I do."

He shrugged as if that was that.

"But—"

"No buts, Philippa," he snapped, whirling around to face her head-on. "You made your decision. I told you what would happen."

She blinked up at him, her lips parting. *You'll be mine forever.*

She swallowed hard. "I thought you meant…" She stopped when his brows fell in anger. "That is, I told you already I could be your mistress."

"And I told you that is unacceptable."

End of conversation. He started to move away, and panic surged, hot and fierce.

"I cannot be a countess," she started, scrabbling forward on the bed, forgetting about modesty as the covers fell away.

"We've been over that. You can and you will." His tone was dismissive as he headed toward the door.

"I won't do it," she said, her voice too loud, causing him to freeze with one hand on the doorknob. He turned back and his expression was shuttered. "You yourself were the first to mention marriage. Don't you recall?"

She did. Back when she'd first arrived, on their way to London. "Yes, but that was…that was before…"

He arched a brow. "Before what?"

Her lips remained parted, but no words came out. Before what? Before she'd seen his kindness. Before he'd made her laugh. Before he'd danced with her and held her in his arms and whispered soft soothing words to her when she was in pain. That was before…before…

Oh hell. That was before she realized she might like him.

When she never finished answering, he turned away with a huff. "Take your time getting ready for the day," he said, his back to her. "Save your energy for tonight."

"Tonight?" She shook her head. Tonight could wait. Throwing all modesty to the wind, she raced across the room, stark naked and terrified.

She could admit it. She was terrified. This wasn't right. It wasn't how this was supposed to go. "I cannot marry you," she said, clinging to his arm like a waif begging on the streets.

His gaze dropped down, taking in her bare breasts, lingering on the dark thatch of curls between her thighs. She went to drop a hand, reflexively trying to shield herself from his gaze, but he caught her wrist in a viselike grip. "Don't," he barked.

Her eyes widened as his gaze met hers. "Mine, remember?"

There was nothing to shield her from his eyes now. Nothing to hide the fact that she was trembling. With panic. With desire. With fear.

"Why do you think you cannot marry me?" he asked.

It was a test. It felt that way, at least. His gaze bore into hers, and she opened her mouth to speak, but her throat wouldn't let her.

"I don't deserve marriage." Not to someone nice, at least. Not to someone who would treat her well.

And he would. Despite what she'd heard, and despite his gruff and rude demeanor, she knew it now as well as she knew her own name.

He would be good to her. And that she did not deserve.

That would be torture she could not bear.

Her hands fell from his arm, and after another silence, she saw a flicker of disappointment in his eyes before he turned away and left her alone, naked and shaking.

CHAPTER THIRTEEN

B ENEDICT SHOULD HAVE known his ward would not go along with his plans without a fight.

He had known it. He'd expected it. But he wasn't about to let her stubborn arse keep him from doing what was right.

"Her mother would be pleased," his mother was muttering as they waited for Philippa to join them in the front hall. "So, at least, there's that."

He ignored her. She'd been muttering asides for the past half hour as they waited. Hell, she'd been expressing her opinions on this match since he'd tracked her down to tell her.

He hadn't expected a happy reaction to the news, but she'd been even more taciturn than ever about this turn of events. She seemingly took it as a personal affront. As if he'd set out to seduce her goddaughter just to aggravate her.

But despite her misgivings about the matter, she'd taken it in stride eventually, thinking through the logistics of a hasty wedding to try and avert any more gossip. As she'd so delicately put it, *Lord knows this family doesn't need to be tainted by any more of your wicked scandals.*

Which was why she was here, ready and waiting to do her part to pretend to be joyous about this upcoming wedding.

She'd decided to spin it as a love story as if anyone would believe that. Well, they might very well believe that he'd become smitten with his ward, but that a sweet, smiling beauty like Philippa would fall for a scarred, bitter beast like him?

No. If anything, she'd likely be getting her fair share of pitying glances at tonight's soiree as his mother spread the news.

He tugged at his cravat again, glaring up at the top of the staircase as if that might make her appear. The carriages were ready and waiting, as he had been for nigh on an hour now. He peered up the spiraling staircase. "Where is she?"

"Maria says she's nearly done," his mother said.

He gave a harrumph. He knew what Philippa was doing. The little vixen was digging in her heels. As if by not attending tonight's event where his mother would undoubtedly announce the good news of their engagement, she might somehow avoid the inevitable.

A muscle in his jaw twitched.

She didn't want him. Not in any meaningful way. And that was fine. He'd never expected her to want him. Hell, after the fire he'd lost any fantasy he might have had of finding a true partner—or even that rare magic that Raff had found.

No, he certainly hadn't been holding out for love.

But knowing he was to marry a woman who hated him, who didn't wish to be seen at his side...

He inhaled swiftly, shaking off the thought.

Perhaps this was justice. He was finally doing the right thing, being the sort of upstanding gentleman his father expected—well, in his own way. And in turn, he'd be despised in his own home.

He glanced over at his mother.

Even more than he already was.

"There you are," his mother said.

His head snapped up, and his breath caught at the sight of her. Breathtaking.

She'd been right. She wasn't meant to be a countess. She ought to be a queen.

Her red hair was swept up in some coif that made it look like she was wearing a crown, and her green eyes sparkled down at him. Her freckles were covered in some sort of powder that made her look ethereal in the candlelight's glow.

"You look lovely, dear," his mother said.

He glanced over at his mother, surprised by the kindness in her tone. It appeared she wasn't going to hold this marriage against Philippa, and he was glad.

They didn't need any more obstacles standing in her way.

Her chin was notched up high when she descended the stairs, and while she made all the polite greetings to his mother, she all but ignored him until he offered his arm to escort her out to the carriage.

"I will not let this happen, you know," she said.

"I don't see how you'll avoid it." He was pleased by how calm he sounded despite the anger brewing in his chest.

"I'll make you regret it," she said, the words low and poisonous. "I'll make a cuckold of you before we even wed, I'll—"

He spun her to face him so quickly, she stopped talking at once.

"Let us be clear, Philippa. I know you do not like this arrangement. But if you were so repulsed by me and dislike me so thoroughly, that is something you ought to have taken into consideration before you invited me into your bed."

Her eyes widened, and she looked stricken.

"Now, how you behave tonight is up to you, of course. But know that you must live with the consequences if you are a naughty girl."

Her flaming cheeks said she knew precisely what he meant, and he felt his cock stir as her pupils dilated, and her lips parted with desire. "You wouldn't."

He didn't answer. He didn't need to.

He'd never in his life lift a hand to a woman in anger, but this was not that, and they both knew it. She'd come apart in his arms when he took control, and she'd only lost those shadows in her eyes when she surrendered to his commands.

With that memory in mind, he leaned down close, sliding a

hand down to cup her bottom in a forceful grip. "You are mine now, love." He gave that plump arse a gentle spank, a tease of what was to come.

She inhaled with a gasp and bit her lip as her gaze grew unfocused with desire.

Lord, but she was tempting.

"Are you wet for me, pet?" he whispered in her ear.

She turned a brilliant shade of red. "Between my thighs, you mean?"

He had to fight a smile. This girl. So very haughty and sophisticated one moment and then a sheltered country girl the next.

"Mmm," he managed, his lips grazing her ear. "If I were to hitch up this pretty gown of yours and slide my hand between your thighs, would your tight little cunny be wet for me?"

Her shiver wracked her whole body. "Yes."

"Good girl," he whispered. He caught her about the waist as she swayed into him. "Now, are you going to behave tonight, or will I have to take you over my knee?"

Despite his threatening growl, she grinned up at him—and the sight nearly took him out at the knees. It was the first real smile he'd seen from her since last night, and it made his heart swell dangerously.

"Careful, Benedict," she said with a wink. "Your threat isn't much of a threat if I enjoy the punishment."

She walked away from him with a saucy little strut that had him scrubbing a hand over his mouth to hide his smile.

He hadn't expected her to be a biddable bride, but he suspected Philippa was going to give new meaning to the term trouble.

"I HEAR CONGRATULATIONS are in order." Raff was beaming with satisfaction as he and his wife joined Benedict by the fireplace in their host's drawing room.

Raff's wife Evangeline greeted him with a soft smile. "We were so happy to hear the news."

"How *did* you hear of it?" he asked, looking around at the crowd that had gathered.

For an intimate soiree, this house was filled to capacity with lords and ladies.

"Word travels fast when an earl becomes engaged," Raff said. "And we wanted to be the first to wish you well. But I had to hear it from you first." Raff arched his brows. "Are we truly celebrating a betrothal?"

"I am, I suppose." He forced a crooked smile for Evangeline's sake. "I'm afraid my bride-to-be is not exactly enthused by this turn of events."

Evangeline winced and squeezed Benedict's arm in support. "Where is she? Perhaps she could use a friend to talk to."

His smile eased into something more genuine. "I'd appreciate that. Last I saw, she was with my mother and her friends, being bombarded with well wishes and ill-disguised interrogations."

Evangeline grimaced. "I can imagine. Poor dear must be overwhelmed."

"Mmm. Poor dear," he muttered under his breath as Evangeline walked away to find Philippa. The fact that his friend's wife didn't ask questions about why, precisely, he was forcing the "poor dear" into a wedding made him like the pretty blonde all the more.

"Care to tell me what's going on?" Raff said.

"Not really."

Raff laughed. "Fair enough."

"What about me?" Hayden approached from behind and apparently had heard enough to guess the topic. "They say I'm much easier to talk to than His Grace over here."

Raff pretended to be offended, and Benedict shook his head in exasperation at his friends' antics.

"Not the time nor the place," he said, looking around them

pointedly.

"Fine, later then perhaps you can explain just how you managed to woo that sweet little Italian lass," Hayden said.

Benedict gave a snort of amusement. Woo? Hardly. But he'd not risk any of these vipers overhearing the truth.

His gaze was searching the crowd for any sight of her—he felt uneasy whenever he didn't have eyes on her—and only half listened as his friends muttered about that bastard Foley being in attendance…again.

"I don't understand how he manages to get an invitation to these events," Hayden grumbled.

Raff arched a brow. "Based on personal experience, I'd say blackmail."

"Hmph." Hayden scowled at no one in particular, but a passing matron smiled brilliantly back at him.

He had the sort of angelic, boyish handsomeness that made women fawn over him, even when he was brooding.

One glance at Benedict had that same matron scurrying away.

"It's time we get word out that he's not welcome," Hayden said.

Hayden was nothing if not a loyal friend, and he'd taken to ensuring Evangeline was comfortable at these gatherings with the same protective air of her husband. Well, not quite the same. Hayden's concern was more brotherly, whereas Raff was known to whisk his wife away for a quick frolic in an empty bedroom.

"I'd be happy to but it's difficult to skewer his good name without tarnishing my wife's," Raff said.

All three of them stewed over that in silence until the crowd shifted, and Philippa came into view. Philippa…and the very man they'd just been discussing.

"The nerve," Benedict bit out through clenched teeth.

His friends turned to see what he was watching.

Raff cursed as well. Understandably as his wife was standing beside a seemingly unaware Philippa, glaring at Mr. Foley like a warrior woman. But Philippa…

Jealousy and rage shot through him so quickly, he was moving before his friends could stop him.

"Easy now," Raff said. "You don't want to cause a scene and embarrass her."

"Embarrass her?" He shot his friend a glare. "What do you think she's doing to me?"

She wasn't just speaking with Foley, she was flirting with him. He could see as much even from where they were standing. Batting her eyelashes and smiling a simpering smile that had his hands clenched at his side. He was a few feet away when she rested a hand against Foley's arm, and Benedict saw red.

"Pardon us," he bit out curtly as he grabbed her hand and dragged her away.

"Benedict, what are you doing?"

But he heard it in her voice. She'd done this on purpose. She knew exactly what she'd been doing. The little minx still thought she could get out of this engagement if she made a fool of him.

He didn't stop moving until they were outside in the cold early spring air. His skin felt feverish as he hauled her into his arms. He didn't wait to hear her protests before he ravished her mouth with a kiss that was as good as a brand.

"Mine." He muttered the word between kisses, his tongue probing, his lips rough, not stopping the onslaught until she was sinking into his chest and moaning into his mouth. Only then did he pull back and when he did, it was to shove his hand into her bodice, gripping one of her breasts and pinching her nipple until she whimpered with need.

"Say it," he demanded.

Her lips quivered, her eyes dazed. "I'm yours."

"Say it like you understand," he snarled.

Her throat moved as she swallowed. "I-I'm yours."

"Forever," he added.

Her eyes grew glazed in that way he adored. The way that said she was losing herself, handing herself into his care. Letting him be the master of her pleasure.

"Forever," she repeated.

"Did you think you could escape me by flirting with another?"

Her eyes widened, a flare of helplessness there. No, she hadn't truly thought it would work, but she'd been desperate enough to try.

Frustration coursed through him at the demons that were eating her alive.

"I cannot help you if you don't let me," he growled. "I cannot take away your pain if you keep it locked inside."

She tossed her head before throwing herself at him with desperation just like she'd done so many times before. Her fingers reached for his manhood as she rubbed herself against his chest, her lips on his neck. "You can take away the pain," she whispered. "Only you know how."

Only you…

The words were more seductive than any touch or smile. It wrapped around him and squeezed his chest.

He moved her deeper into the shadows, hidden from sight because…what the hell. They were engaged now. Propriety be damned. He pushed her back against a tree in the garden.

"Please, Benedict," she whimpered. "I need you."

He hitched up her skirts and tore her undergarments. *Mine.* The word was an incessant chant, and it drove his every move. He didn't need Foley to know it. He didn't care if anyone else understood.

All that mattered was that she realized he would never let her go. No matter what she did. No matter how miserable she made him.

"Yes," she hissed, her eyes alight with desperation and need.

He dropped to his knees first, parting the fabric of her undergarments with a groan. "So wet," he whispered.

"It hurts," she whimpered. Her hips jutted forward.

He buried his face between her thighs, groaning again as she gasped above him, her sweet, wet heat ready for him. Her fingers tangled in his hair, and she jerked her hips. "What are you…How is this…"

She stopped trying to talk as he drove his tongue into her channel, making her knees quake.

He shoved her thighs apart further and angled his head so his mouth could cover her whole mound at once.

He was so hungry for her, his bollocks ached for more. She tasted like…well, like Philippa. Wild and sweet, wanton and innocent. She was perfection, and when she moved her hips, trying to find her release, he found himself grinning against her sex.

The jealousy was forgotten because of this… This was for him alone.

Whether she liked it or not, he was the only man who'd ever taste this nectar, and it was his own private heaven. He growled against her, flicking her clitoris with his tongue as she panted and moaned.

"You like that, love?" he teased. "You want more?"

Her hands in his hair grew frantic as she rode his face like the marvelous little spitfire she was.

"More," she panted. "More."

He thrust his tongue inside her again, his hands cupping her bottom. He gave one cheek a sharp slap, and he felt her inner muscles clench around his tongue.

She was a wonder.

He did it again, smacking her bottom hard and then harder still as she begged for more, her legs spread wide as she sat on his face and took all he had to offer.

She came with a shout, and he lapped at her until she was shaking. Then he stood and in two swift movements, he had his manhood out and buried inside her, pinning her to the tree as he drove into her.

Her head fell back with a pant. "Yes," she gasped. "Yes, please."

He buried his neck in her hair. He was an animal, scarred, ugly, and coarse. And this proved it. There was no finesse, just a hard, rough tupping as he made his sweet bride-to-be take all of him inside her.

"Good," she panted. "Feels so good."

The words rippled over him, making him shudder as heat shot down his spine and into his loins. She liked it. Even rutting with her like the animal he was, she liked it.

"Perfect," he growled into her ear as he slid his length into her. "So bloody perfect."

Now she was shivering as he drove inside of her, thrusting into her like he could make her see what she meant to him. What this could be.

Her legs clamped around his waist; her arms cinched around his neck. She squeezed him tight.

He came apart with a groan, and for a long moment, they stayed just like that, trembling and panting as they returned to reality.

"Was that supposed to be a punishment?" Even breathless and shaking, she managed to taunt.

He grunted. "A reminder of who you belong to." He shot her a warning glare, just in case she thought he'd forgotten that she'd been flirting with the enemy not ten minutes prior.

She shrugged but looked away. "I told you I'd make you regret it."

He caught it then—another flicker of hate in her eyes. But it wasn't toward him, and that knowledge just about ripped him apart. "Tell me what happened," he said.

It was a command.

She couldn't resist commands, his naughty little bird.

"I said you belong to me," he growled. "But haven't you figured it out yet, love? This thing between us—the vows we've already made. The acts we've already committed…"

Her lips parted at the urgency in his voice, and he saw tears lining her eyes.

He wet his lips. This moment felt heavy and fragile at the same time. Words had never been his strong suit, but this felt like the most obvious fact in the world. "Philippa, you belong to me. But I am yours now, too. Do you not see that?"

She blinked in surprise.

"We are one now, love. We are on the same side."

She shook her head, not in refusal, but in pain. Like she was trying to shake off his words. "You cannot be shackled to me," she said. "It isn't right. You deserve better."

He froze so completely, he nearly forgot to breathe. Here he'd been so certain she didn't want to be tied to his scarred, ugly arse, but...

"You think you are not deserving?" he said. "Of me?"

She shut her eyes.

"Of what?" He cupped her cheek. "Of what are you not deserving, love?"

"Don't call me that." Her eyes snapped open. "Don't call me love."

"Why not?"

Her throat worked as she swallowed. "I should not get...this." She gestured helplessly.

He frowned in confusion. "Not get what?"

She shook her head quickly again, making a production out of straightening her clothes.

"Not get what, Philippa?" His voice was harder now, his patience thin.

"This." Her voice rose with anguish, her control slipping. "The good man. The happy ending. A bloody title, for heaven's sake." Her exhale was somewhere between a harsh laugh and a desperate sob.

He went to reach for her. "Why not?"

"I need to pay, don't you see?" Her eyes were wild, her voice high and tight as her hands waved between them beseechingly. "I'm supposed to be punished for what I've done. I'm not supposed to be pitied." She cast a glance toward the house where all of high society was blissfully unaware of what they'd just done. "I'm not supposed to be happy." She looked to him. "I should be punished."

"Punished." The word tasted bitter on his tongue. She'd said it before, but now it took on new meaning. She didn't mean a spanking for making him jealous or anything else as inconsequential. "For what?"

"For killing my parents, Benedict." The anguish in her voice made his own heart hurt. "I must pay for what I've done, don't you see?"

He went to reach for her, but she turned away from him, but not before he'd seen her tears.

CHAPTER FOURTEEN

P HILIPPA WAS HARDLY aware of how she got home, only that
Benedict's caring was unbearable.

When had he become such a gentle giant? This wasn't how
he was supposed to be.

But as he made their excuses—as he told his mother he'd
send another carriage for her and bid farewell to his friends—the
truth was unavoidable.

He was too damned kind.

The moment she was in the carriage she shook off his firm
but gentle helping hand and settled into her seat. It was a churlish
gesture and she knew it.

Benedict did not take the seat across from her. Instead, he
forced his large body onto the bench beside her as the carriage
jolted into motion, and before she could so much as protest, he
dragged her into his lap. His hands were firm on her hips. Even
through the thick fabric of her gown, she could feel him holding
her in place.

She forced herself to sit upright, ignoring the comfort his
body was offering as the carriage rocked and jerked its way down
the cobblestone street toward Benedict's townhome.

Silence filled the small space as she waited for the questions to
begin.

One cannot simply admit to murdering one's parents without

expecting a whole host of questions.

But Benedict stayed just as silent as she, though his gaze never left her profile. She could feel the heat of his stare as she kept her eyes trained on the darkness outside the carriage window.

Once home, the excruciating kindness continued as Benedict dispatched of the servants, telling them their services would not be needed that night.

Perhaps she ought to be embarrassed as he led her up the stairs to her bedroom. They must know who would be helping her to undress. Who would be in her room tonight.

But she couldn't bring herself to be embarrassed. This hollow feeling inside of her persisted. It had ever since she'd spoken the words aloud.

He did not stop at her door, instead guiding her by the arm to continue down the hallway, not stopping until they reached his bedroom door.

"You'll stay here tonight," he said, finally breaking the long silence between them to issue this one command.

She nodded, some part of her already resigned to what was to come. But she didn't fight it, not even when his touch made her want to scream as he slowly unfastened her gown, as he gently tugged the pins free from her hair.

He did not stop until she was sheathed in nothing but her chemise and stockings, her hair long and loose around her shoulders.

Cupping her face in his hands, he leaned down until his nose grazed hers. "So beautiful," he murmured against her lips.

She opened for him, craving the taste of him, even as the rest of her slumbered in a numb state that ought to be terrifying.

But it wasn't. It was a relief. It was a temporary stay, and she meant to enjoy it. So, she kissed him back slowly, letting his lips guide her as she learned what he liked. What she liked.

It was nothing like the messy, passionate, dirty affair back in the garden. This slow kiss, the way he'd so gently disrobed her…

This was what it would have been like if she truly were an innocent, and this her wedding night. She lost all sense of time as his lips moved with hers, teasing and claiming, nipping and caressing. Her mind was a blissful blank when he broke the kiss briefly to scoop her up into his arms, cradling her tight as he took her over to the bed.

He set her down so gently as if she were made of glass and might shatter in his hands.

His tenderness was too much. Tears welled in her eyes as he sank down onto the mattress beside her. He saw the tears. Of course he did. When it came to her, she was certain there was nothing this man did not see.

But rather than pester her with questions or demand explanations, he kissed her tears away, making her breath hitch as his body came over hers, blocking out the rest of the room...the rest of the world.

With seemingly endless patience, he kissed her cheeks, her jaw, her neck, her eyelids. Such light kisses for a man so big and strong.

His scars were a reassurance whenever they brushed her skin. With her eyes shut, they were a calling card, a reminder. He's been through pain, too. He knew grief. He understood guilt.

Not the same though. This much, she knew. He might have his share of regrets, but it was not the same.

But for now...for tonight...

It was enough.

And when he slid over her, his body a solid, grounding weight that made her sink into the mattress as a delicious heat curled through her veins...

That was more than enough. It was everything.

The world came down to his touch. Her mind was set free as sensations took over. It was all so very different from the night before. There were no secrets and no lies. There was no punishment and no deceit, no taunts and no commands.

There were gasps and moans as his rough, scarred chest

moved over the tender skin of her breasts. The sound of her own labored breathing filled her ears as his mouth explored every inch of her, leisurely and with the utmost care.

She watched the shadows from the candlelight flicker on the ceiling above as he tasted her again like he had out in the garden earlier. But this time he was so very gentle that she thought she might scream.

In the end, she did scream when he slid his fingers inside her as he sucked on that hard nub and made her shatter, leaving the harsh world far behind as a giddy, intoxicating joy flooded her body from head to toe.

Only then did he move up, covering her again with his body—a hot, weighty sensation that made her heart ache for no reason she could explain except that it made her feel safe in a way she hadn't since…since she couldn't remember when.

His body was so large that he swallowed her up as he loomed over her, and when he fitted himself between her thighs, that hard shaft nudging at her core, her eyes fluttered shut, and her lips parted in ecstasy. The feel of it was so very right, so very comforting.

She felt cherished and protected, and when his hard length pushed inside of her, she clung to him, wanting him even closer still. Needing him inside of her and around her.

She wanted to be consumed by him because that was the only time she felt sane and whole and…loved.

A gasp slipped out at the thought, but Benedict swallowed the sound with a kiss that soothed her.

She pushed the thought aside and focused on this feeling instead, letting herself drown in the sensation of him inside her, filling her up so completely it came just short of pain. Of him surrounding her so thoroughly that her every sense was filled with him, from his clean, masculine scent, to the rough, hot touch of his skin.

His movements were slow and even as he thrust in and out. There was no rush, no urgency as they reveled in the feel of it. If anything, she suspected he was drawing it out, stopping when one of them came too close to climaxing until she thought she might scream with the need to find a release.

Finally, when they were both covered in sweat, when her hips arched jerky and frantic, only then did he finally give her what she craved. What she needed. He lifted her knees, his gaze locked on hers as he drove inside of her, finding that spot that made her gasp and stroking it over and over until she tossed her head back with a cry.

He groaned a short time after, his seed spurting inside of her as he tensed all over. And when he was done, he pulled out slowly and dragged her into his arms.

With her back to his chest, she could feel his scars as well as his heartbeat as he nuzzled the back of her neck, so gently she giggled. "That tickles," she whispered.

She could feel his smile against her shoulder.

Philippa wasn't certain how much time passed like that as she drifted between this blissful satiated state and light sleep. It was heaven on earth.

Which meant she should have known it couldn't last.

"You'll have to tell me eventually, you know," he said.

He didn't sound angry. Not even impatient or frustrated. His hand stroked her hip when she tensed, and soon, he was stroking her like a kitten.

She had to resist the urge to purr as she pushed back against him, eager for more.

He stroked her until every muscle was loose and languid, and she found that delicious place again between heaven and sleep.

The candles had flickered out, and she stared into the dark with heavy-lidded eyes. He was so quiet, it was only the soft, consistent movement of his hand on her skin that made it clear he had not drifted off.

And without any prompting, without a single question, she found herself talking, the sordid tale falling from her lips like it was someone else's story. Like it was someone else's life.

"I've never been a good girl," she started.

His hand stilled, but after a heartbeat, he resumed the soft, rhythmic caress. She focused on that, on the touch of his scarred hand against her skin as the words came out as if they'd been there all along just waiting to be freed.

"I don't know why. It's not like I didn't try. I wanted to be good. I wanted to please my mother and to make my father proud. But no matter how hard I tried, I was always trouble."

He didn't speak but he shifted even closer until every inch of her was pressed against him like he could take on her pain by sheer proximity.

"If I hadn't been baptized, my father likely would have blamed my bad behavior on an evil spirit. As it was, he believed there to be something wrong with me."

His grip tightened on her hip for a heartbeat, and she heard his hard swallow.

She took a deep breath and let it out with a sigh, her mind already going backward in time until it was all there, fresh in her mind. "My mother tried her best to teach me how to be a proper young lady so that one day I might fit into English society. That was always her dream for me, you know. Ever since she'd gone to that finishing school with your mother, she'd dreamt that I might marry into the *ton*." She shook her head. She'd lost focus. "So, my mother was not to blame for my bad behavior, and my father tried his best to beat it out of me—"

She stopped when he went rigid behind her. But, like he knew she wouldn't continue if he were to speak, he got control over himself and went back to the hypnotic caressing, though she could feel his heart pounding hard.

Once again, she changed tack. Her parents weren't to blame. These were her sins she was confessing. "I'd always loved to ride. Being in the stables with the horses or riding bareback out in the woods behind our property, those were the only times I felt free." She took a deep breath. "I fell in love with the stable boy."

Now he didn't just still, he stopped breathing, and his every muscle turned to stone.

But he did not speak, and she forced herself to hurry on, unable to hide the bitterness in her tone. "At least, I thought it was love at the time. I thought he understood me. I thought he was my salvation. I would flee the stifling tension in my house and seek him out in the stables and..." She trailed off. "Anyway, I was wrong."

Benedict's hand wrapped around her waist and squeezed.

"He did not love me. He only wanted what he thought I would give freely because word had spread, of course, that I was a wicked, wicked girl. My father found these salacious, lewd books I'd stolen, you see..." She swallowed hard. It didn't matter. "What I thought was love and romance was merely seduction. You see, I wasn't quite as wanton back then. I was curious and smitten, and I let him touch me. But as you know, I'm a nasty tease. That was what he called me eventually. Just a wicked, nasty tease."

Even she could hear the jaded, harsh note in her voice, and she cleared her throat.

"I thought I was in love but I was a fool." That was the long and short of it. "My father discovered that we'd been meeting in secret, and he was furious, of course."

She tried to calm her racing heart, to even out her unsteady breathing as the memories of his rage surfaced, the way he'd smacked her and tossed her to the ground. Her mother hadn't even tried to intervene as he'd raged about her evil nature and how it needed to be beaten out of her.

She hadn't tried to protest either because... even then she'd known that perhaps he was right. "I realized then that there was no fixing me. There was no cure for my wickedness."

His breathing was short and choppy in her ear. He sounded like he was trying for calm, too.

"I ran away," she said. "Or...or I tried to."

She had to swallow twice to get the next part out. "I thought he would run with me. The stable boy, I mean. I hadn't realized yet that there were no real feelings there, just a game on his part to get between my legs. I thought…I thought we were in it together, so to speak."

Benedict's hand was a reassuring weight, holding her still and letting her know she was here, now. Not back in the past.

"But when I showed up at the stables, weeping and talking of fleeing my family, he laughed at me and told me quite plainly what he'd been after and what he thought of me."

A growl slipped out of Benedict, and she had the ridiculous urge to soothe him, so she added, "It wasn't really his fault. I was the fool for having such childish, romantic notions. I should have known better."

He didn't argue, but she could feel tension radiating from his too-still body behind her.

"I left without him, but he must have told my father where I was going. In hindsight, I realized that, of course, he would do whatever he could to regain some favor with my father. He'd need a reference, after all, to find another job and—"

"Philippa, love," Benedict interrupted her babbling. He kissed the back of her head and then her temple.

You're here, his touch seemed to say. *You're safe.*

She took a deep, shaky breath. "My parents followed in my wake. My father must have been furious, and no doubt my mother wished to come along to try and spare me the worst of his anger." She stopped to swallow. "It was raining. The roads in our part were slick and dangerous even during the best weather. The bridge was flooded, a fact I knew, but I made my horse keep going all the same." Her breathing was growing too short and uneven. "I knew they were behind me. I knew my father wouldn't stop chasing me just because of some water. Nothing could stop my father when he was in a temper."

She paused, her heart beating so loudly she could barely hear her own voice. "I led them straight into danger and…and then…and then…"

She couldn't say it.

She had to say it.

"I led them straight to their death."

The words rang in the air, echoing back to her. For the first time since that night, she wept. She sobbed, mourning at all that had been lost in an instant. Grieving for the wicked girl she'd been before and the cruel woman she'd become.

"I tried to save them," she said. "But I couldn't. I killed them." She repeated it in her sobs, so many times she must have sounded like a lunatic.

But Benedict kept holding her, tighter and tighter each time she said it. Like he could make it untrue by sheer force.

And then he was turning her over, kissing her tears away again, but this time with urgent, harsh kisses. And in between, he was growling all the words she'd wanted to hear these past years.

It's not your fault. You were not to blame. It was an accident.

Such sweet, kind, wonderful words. Such tempting thoughts. It all sounded so nice. Reasonable, even, when it came from a man so commanding as he.

He had a way of making everything sound so true and right. His word was law, and he would not let her take the blame.

Benedict was offering her redemption.

"I understand, love," he whispered. "I know what it is to feel guilt. But it was an accident. You cannot blame yourself for something out of your control."

She nodded against his chest as he stroked her hair until sleep threatened to draw her under.

She understood what he was saying, and even how he'd felt the same with his own tragedy.

But it wasn't the same. He'd been negligent in bringing that woman into their home. But there was no way he could have foreseen what would happen. He'd been careless and unthinking, but that was not the same.

She'd known she was leading them into danger. She'd had that wild sensation coursing through her, and she'd known that she was tempting fate.

It was her own life she'd thought she was risking as she rode her horse at a breakneck speed along sharp curves and over that flooded bridge. It was her own life she'd meant to threaten, but it was her parents who paid for her reckless, unthinking, selfish ways that night.

She put her hand over his as he curled his body around her, his arm a weight around her waist. Her heart ached with tenderness for this man who thought he could save her from the hell she'd created.

But he couldn't.

Benedict deserved a second chance. A new beginning.

There was no redemption for her.

CHAPTER FIFTEEN

B ENEDICT'S HEART WAS still heavy two days later on Philippa's behalf.

Her story had shifted his whole world. He'd come to care for her—how and when he wasn't certain, but he'd known it when he'd taken her into his arms that night after she'd bared her heart and soul. He understood then that, even if their circumstances were different... Even if they hadn't been intimate and she wasn't living under his roof....

He'd still want her for his wife.

He'd always want her.

She belonged with him.

"Will Philippa be joining us?" His mother's voice was cold as always, formal, as she faced him over the dining room table.

"I do not know." He hated having to say it. But he'd given Philippa the space she so clearly needed these past two days, respecting the fact that she needed time to herself after the emotional upheaval of her confession.

"She did not join us last night," his mother mused, her tone toxic. "I hope she has not taken ill."

His hands tightened into fists as the servants brought out the first course. His mother had decided to take her meals with him since their arrival in town, likely because the townhouse wasn't as spacious as the country estate and to avoid one another here would be difficult.

"I'm sure she is fine, Mother," he said.

Another silence fell as the servants left, only a footman waiting next to the door should they need him.

Benedict wasn't at all sure she was fine, but he had no idea what else to do for her. He'd attempted to draw her out of her rooms, offering to escort her through the park and inviting her to join him for meals, but she'd quietly and politely refused him.

He scowled down at his meal now. He didn't like a quiet and polite Philippa. That wasn't her nature. He missed her teasing and her impulsive, outrageous comments. He missed her laughter when she'd goaded him into a growl.

Hell, he missed *her*.

He stared at the door like she might suddenly materialize.

"Her mother did say she was spoiled," his mother said with a little *tsk* of judgment. "I suppose she's pouting because we have not thrown a proper engagement party yet."

Benedict stared at his mother for a long moment. His bride-to-be was suffering right now, and his mother thought she was pouting?

His mother arched a brow as she glanced up at him. "Or perhaps she's moping because you've forced her into being a countess?" She sniffed. "I can think of worse fates for a foreign girl with no connections to speak of."

He shook his head in disgust at the assumptions she was making, the aspersions she was casting. "You do not know of what you speak."

"Don't I?" She gave a humorless laugh. "I saw the way you two have been looking at one another since the moment she arrived. I'd say I pity the girl for having caught your fancy, but I daresay she was just as smitten."

He clenched his jaw and looked down at his food. He didn't need a mirror nearby to know what he looked like. He could feel the taut pull of his disfigured skin. "We both know that's not true."

His mother's soft snort of disdainful amusement had him glancing up. She reached for her wine glass. "Don't tell me you were so caught up in self-pity you did not notice." She narrowed her eyes and studied him critically. "Those scars might have marred your handsome features, but I daresay there are women out there who are drawn to the dark and the ugly."

His hand stilled as he reached for a glass of his own. "Thank you, Mother. As always, your words of wisdom are a comfort to us all."

"Oh, don't be droll," she snapped. "I only speak the truth."

But she hadn't said whatever it was she wished to say, this much he knew from experience. He leaned back and crossed his arms over his chest, dipping his chin to level her with an even stare. "Go on then. Say whatever it is you want to say."

For a moment she just stared. But then her lips quivered and her nostrils flared. "How is it just that you get the happy ending? After all the tragedy you've caused, and here you sit, the lord of his castle with a sweet, beautiful bride and all the power and wealth you could ask for."

The words spewed out of her mouth. "You don't deserve a wife and children, the family your brother ought to have."

When he made no move to defend himself, when he merely sat there and listened, it went on and on until he was sure he could see her exhaustion.

Heavy as his heart was to hear her vengeful, angry, spiteful words, he understood that exhaustion. It was tiring to carry that sort of anger around.

"You never wanted this," she said, gesturing around them.

And she was right. He never had. This was his brother's life he was living, and he well knew it. All he'd wanted was the independence that came with being the younger son. All he'd cared about was having his independence, chafing anytime family obligations stifled his freedom.

"You're right," he said when it became clear that she was done. "I never wanted this life, and Lord knows I don't deserve it.

If there was any way I could bring them back, I would." He met his mother's gaze evenly. So much had been made clear to him as he'd listened to Phillippa's heartache and anguish.

"Mother, if I could trade my life for theirs, I would."

Her lips trembled again, but this time not with anger.

"But I cannot." He gave a helpless shrug. "And this is my life, whether either of us likes it or not."

For a long moment, the only sound in the room was their breathing.

His jaw worked for a long moment. "Mother…" He cleared his throat. He'd never said it. He'd never said the words she needed to hear. The words he had to say. "I'm sorry."

"That's not enough," she hissed, but there were tears in her eyes as well as anger.

"I know it's not enough, but it still needs to be said." He swallowed hard. "I am sorry for the mistakes I made that led to their deaths. I'm sorry for every harsh word I ever said to either of them, for every drink I had that night that left me useless when my family needed me most. I'm sorry for Francesca—"

"Do not say her name," his mother shouted.

"I'm sorry I brought her into our home. I'm sorry for all of it, Mother. But it's time we stop avoiding the conversation. We can't keep pretending it never happened—"

"I'm not—"

"You hate me for it," he continued. "And I understand that."

She didn't deny it.

"I hate myself for all that happened," he said. Another long silence passed as they both sat with their thoughts. He didn't know where his mother's mind went, but his thoughts were with Philippa. Right now, he ached to be at her side.

She was pushing him away, and he couldn't let that continue.

He'd given her space, but now it was time. It was time for them both to forgive their pasts and move forward.

"I'm about to start a new life, Mother," he said. "With Philippa. And I hope with you, as well."

Her brows arched slightly in surprise.

"I hope you will be a part of our lives because I mean to move forward. I mean to make of this earldom what father would have wanted. My brother, too."

She pressed her lips together with a sniff.

"Philippa is a good woman. I know you do not approve the match, and maybe you don't approve of her—"

"Nonsense," she snapped. "I love that girl. She reminds me of her mother."

"Does she?" He thought back to what Philippa said. "Does she know that?"

"What do you mean?"

"I mean…" He cleared his throat. This was not a conversation for him to be having with his mother. "I mean, I think she could use your help, Mother. She will definitely need your guidance, and if you could manage to let go of some of your hatred and your anger—not at me," he added quickly when she stiffened. "I don't expect you to forgive me. But if you could put aside your anger long enough to show her love, maybe you and I can both find a way to move forward."

She stared down at her food but made no move to eat. When he thought she would never respond at all, she finally spoke. "I do not hate you, Benedict."

His heart clenched, but he didn't dare speak.

"You are my child, and I could never hate you. I'm just…I've just been so angry." Her voice shook, and he reached across the table to touch her hand.

"I know."

She lifted her gaze, and he saw a world of pain in her eyes. "I'm still so angry."

He nodded. He knew that, too.

"But you are right," she continued, her voice returning to normal. "We owe it to them both to make this family whole again."

"Thank you, Mother."

After dinner, he headed up to Philippa's room. He understood her need to grieve alone, but he'd meant what he'd said. This was their chance—it was a chance for all of them to move forward. To forgive and to heal.

He knocked on her door and let himself in when there was no answer.

Philippa was stretched out on her bed, just as she had been the last time he'd checked on her. He sat beside her and touched her hand. "Have you had any food?"

"I'm not hungry."

He itched to argue. Part of him wondered if barking commands would work at a time like this...but he didn't think so.

She'd never admit it aloud, but his wife-to-be needed tenderness now. He laid down beside her on his side, resting a hand on her belly. "You cannot stay in here forever, you know."

Her smile was small and sad. "I know. I just..." She shook her head. "Saying it all aloud like that..."

He nodded. "No one else knows."

She shook her head, even though it wasn't a question. He leaned forward and kissed her temple. He had a feeling that was the hardest part for her.

He'd had his mother's wrath, the whispers of the *ton*, not to mention the horrid scars he'd faced every day in the mirror. He'd been cast into hell after the accident and had been hated and spurned for his sins.

She'd had nothing but sympathy and kindness, and he imagined that had only made her guilt and shame fester and grow.

No wonder she'd turned to him for punishment.

He winced at the thought, but he did not judge her for it.

She'd seen him as the devil she deserved. And now here she was, trapped in his prison.

He swallowed hard and shoved the thought away as he toyed with her long locks. The time for anger and blame was over now.

He just had to make her see that.

"We could be happy, you know."

For a second, he wasn't sure if she'd heard. But then, as she blinked up at the ceiling, he caught the tear that slid down her cheek. "Do you really think so?" she whispered.

He kissed her softly. "I do. I think we've all made mistakes. You, me, even my mother, and most definitely your parents."

She shot him a glare that he ignored. But truly, if they'd survived that carriage incident, he would have murdered her father himself for taking a hand to her. For convincing her she was anything less than perfect.

He caught her chin and forced her to look at him. "We can be happy. No one is asking you to forget, but it's time we all move on, love. Can you do that for me? For us?"

She blinked at him as if her gaze was just now taking him in. "I'm so tired, Benedict."

He nodded, lying down beside her once more. "I know, love. Get some rest."

She turned her head, and they were so close their noses touched.

He stroked her cheek. "Rest tonight and take some time to put your memories where they belong. In the past. And tomorrow, you will rejoin the living."

Her lips quirked up at the corners, a pale imitation of her brilliant smile. "The masquerade?"

"Mmm. Evangeline will be there, and she'll never forgive me if I don't bring you along."

She laughed softly. "She seems sweet."

He nodded. "And I think she's rather desperate to make a friend of you. She doesn't have any young lady friends among the *ton*."

Philippa's gaze took him in, and her lips curved up a little more. Her voice was light if a little forced. "Then I suppose I'd better attend. I could use a friend myself."

He saw the sadness still in her eyes, heard the strain in her tone. But he grinned as he pressed another kiss to her lips.

She might not be healed yet, but it was a start.

Tomorrow marked a new beginning for all of them.

CHAPTER SIXTEEN

T HE MASK WAS so very fitting. Philippa adjusted it once more, giving Benedict what she hoped was a reassuring smile from where he stood talking to his friends Raff and Hayden.

"I haven't known Lord Foster for long," Evangeline was saying from beside her. "But I've never seen him so happy."

Philippa's smile for Benedict's sake faltered. "You think he's happy?"

Evangeline cut her a penetrating look. "Of course. Just look at the way he's watching over you." She laughed. "I don't think he's taken his eyes off you once."

She chuckled. "Yes, well, that's just because he's waiting for me to cause trouble."

Evangeline's grin held more than a little mischief. "And my husband is just waiting for a moment to steal me away."

Philippa cast her a sidelong look. The more time she spent in Evangeline's presence, the more she liked the girl. She might look like an angel with her white-blonde hair and her beatific demeanor, but there was so much more beneath the surface.

Just like with Benedict. She eyed her betrothed now, and as always, felt a shiver of awareness caress her spine. Beneath his growls and his scars, he was so very caring.

He had so much love to give. She bit her lip. To the right woman.

To the woman who deserved it.

Evangeline's sigh brought her back to the moment, and she followed the other woman's gaze to a now-familiar gentleman. The sight of Mr. Foley made her lips twitch with mirth. All she'd had to do was smile at the man, and Benedict had lost his senses.

The memory of how he'd punished her for flirting with his enemy was enough to have her clenching her thighs together to alleviate the ache.

Benedict had barely touched her since the night she'd told him her secrets. She knew why, of course. He was being thoughtful. Sweet, even.

She looked around them at the judgmental old biddies who seemed to delight in finding fault with Benedict. None of them could guess just how gentle he could be. All they saw were the scars. All they knew were the whispers of his guilt.

Sometimes she envied him his scars.

But tonight, all she could muster was anger on his behalf. He deserved so much better than this.

He deserves so much better than you.

"Do be careful around him," Evangeline was saying.

It took Philippa a moment to realize Evangeline was still watching Foley. Her words of caution brought back the memory of Benedict's command to steer clear of the gentleman.

"Careful? Why? He seems harmless enough." Indeed, the fellow was handsome in a sort of bland, forgettable sort of way. He was smiling now, laughing amiably along with a handful of older women.

Evangeline's lips pressed into a thin line as she watched alongside Philippa.

"What has he done that's so very awful?" Philippa asked. "Benedict would not say."

Evangeline's tight-lipped expression softened, and her tone was rueful. "No, he wouldn't. He and Hayden have been as good a friend to me as they have been to Raff all these years."

Philippa turned to her in surprise. "So, this Mr. Foley harmed you in some way?"

"He tried." Evangeline glared at the man. "I was so sheltered and naive before I met Raff that I actually believed Foley was in love with me."

Philippa winced at the bitterness in the kind girl's tone.

Evangeline sighed. "Fortunately for me, Raff stole me away before I could learn the truth the hard way."

"And the truth was…" Philippa prompted.

Evangeline's expression hardened. "Foley is a fortune seeker, nothing more. Which wouldn't be so horrible." She cast Philippa another wry smile. "Half the *ton* is filled with them."

Philippa laughed at Evangeline's tone. Yes, the more she got to know Evangeline, the more she was certain they could be dear friends.

If she were to stay.

All at once, she could see it. She and Benedict, laughing and kissing. She and Benedict attending parties like this one, surrounded by friends. She and Benedict with children underfoot…

Her lungs hitched at the onslaught of happy images dancing before her.

They could be happy.

She could be happy.

And all at once, the crushing weight of guilt was back. It hadn't ever fully left, she supposed. But with Benedict's strict orders earlier tonight that she get dressed and be ready…

It had been pushed aside. But now it was back, and she was certain it would never truly be gone. It would always be there, pushing her to be self-destructive, keeping her from real happiness.

Keeping Benedict from the happiness he deserved.

"…that's why Raff and the others keep an eye on him," Philippa was saying. "He might not have succeeded in fooling me, but that's only because Raff intervened. If he hadn't…" Evangeline gave a delicate shudder. "I hate to think what might have become of me."

Philippa followed her gaze back to Foley, but her mind was back within the stables. "Yes," she murmured. "I know a thing or two about being gullible in the face of a charming young man."

Evangeline looked at her but didn't ask questions.

Truly, she would be the most wonderful sort of friend.

If she were to stay.

And she was back to that again. It was a thought that had been growing with each passing day, ever since Benedict had listened to her story and offered her redemption.

Redemption and a new life. A good life.

She'd known even as he'd held her that she couldn't accept, as tempting as it might be.

He thought he understood—and indeed, in many ways, he likely did understand more than most. But their mistakes weren't the same. The level of guilt and responsibility was not equal.

She was glad for him that he could move on, but that sort of forgiveness was not meant for her.

"Mark my words," Evangeline said, her voice low with warning. "One of these days, Foley will find a girl all too eager to run off with him. He'll get his fortune, and that poor girl will be doomed to her own personal hell."

Philippa made a noise, a murmur of acknowledgment. But her mind was spinning, her gaze locked on this notorious fortune hunter.

She had a fortune, after all.

And she deserved her own personal hell.

WHEN THE DUKE of Raffian claimed his bride for a turn about the room, which somehow ended in them disappearing for nearly an hour, Philippa found her opportunity to confront the infamous fortune hunter.

Benedict and Hayden were deep in conversation with the Earl

of Fallenmore and his lady, and Philippa found herself pausing beside the utterly forgettable-looking cad she'd been warned about.

"Mr. Foley," she said simply.

"Ah, what a pleasure it is to see you again," he said. And for a moment, Philippa could see how a sheltered young girl might be taken in by such a man. Precisely because he was so average. There was nothing intimidating about him, nor too charming, nor handsome.

He seemed harmless. And that right there was no doubt what made him so insidious.

She allowed the small talk to go on for only a moment longer, bristling with impatience now that she knew him for what he was.

"Shall we dispense with the pleasantries, Mr. Foley," she finally interrupted.

His brows arched slightly, but a keen intelligence sparked in his eyes as he studied her. "Very well. Was there something in particular you wished to discuss..." His sharp eyes flickered over toward Benedict and others. "While your betrothed is otherwise occupied?"

There were others around. Her speaking to him was in no way improper. And yet guilt and shame oozed into her veins.

Was she doing this?

Was she truly doing this?

She watched Benedict's harsh mouth curve up on one corner at something Lord Fallenmore said, and her heart gave a brutal kick.

She turned back to Mr. Foley. "I hear you are a man in need of a fortune, sir."

His eyes narrowed, his expression guarded, but there was no denying the interest there as well. "Are you so very unhappy with your current...predicament?" He cast another meaningful glance toward Benedict, which left her cold.

Was she unhappy with him? No. Quite the contrary. But this

man would never understand that. She didn't answer him outright. "I've also heard that you have a penchant for stealing away unhappy young brides."

His eyes gleamed with renewed interest as a weaslley smile spread across his features. "I am always happy to help a young lady in need."

She tried to smile in return and failed. "Then it seems you and I have much to discuss."

In what seemed like no time at all, it was done. Her new fate was sealed.

By the time Benedict helped her into the carriage, Philippa's future was clear. She'd thought perhaps there'd be some relief in that, in finally knowing how she would pay for her sins.

But all she felt was empty as Benedict climbed in after her and settled into his seat. "Philippa…" He drew her name out in that low growl of his.

She blinked up at him sweetly. "Yes, Benedict?"

"What were you doing talking to Foley for so long?" There was a chiding to his voice, but he didn't sound jealous.

Perhaps he thought she was taunting him again, teasing him into another stolen, passionate encounter.

She swallowed hard, keeping her smile in place. She'd known she wouldn't have long, of course. But Foley was nothing if not quick-witted. He'd understood what she was offering instantly, and a plan had been formed before Benedict could swoop in and hurry her away.

Which he had, whisking her onto the dance floor and not letting her go from his side for the remainder of the night.

But the deed was done. Not even this fearsome warrior could stop it now.

She settled back in her seat. "I feel sorry for the man, if you must know."

His brows lowered. "You're lying."

She shrugged. She *was* lying. One short conversation with the knave was enough to turn her stomach. His charm was skin-deep, and it had disappeared in a heartbeat once she'd spoken plainly.

But he was a means to an end, that was all.

A way out of this engagement Benedict had forced upon her. He'd be humiliated by the scandal, but that couldn't be helped. It was better than being trapped with her for a lifetime.

Benedict's brows were drawing together, and she could all but see the questions forming on his tongue.

She acted swiftly, dropping to her knees the moment the carriage began to move.

His eyes widened. "What are you doing?"

But this was surely obvious as she reached for the fastening of his trousers, her mouth watering for a taste of him. Her blood was rushing through her veins, and a frantic desperation was clawing at her chest as a new realization set in—her time was running out.

"Philippa," he breathed, his hand settling over hers. "You don't have to do this—"

"I want to," she said. "Please, my lord."

His eyes darkened. He couldn't resist her when she was on her knees. Maybe it was wrong, but just being in this position, between his powerful thighs, and at his mercy…

It had her nipples tightening and her sex growing wet.

Tonight. She had tonight to show him how grateful she was—no, that wasn't right. It wasn't gratitude for his kindness that she felt. It was…

She shook her head. There'd be endless time ahead of her to sort through her feelings for this man who'd challenged her and pushed her, cherished her and saved her.

But for tonight, she meant to show him what was in her heart even if she could not put it into words.

Her fingers were clumsy with eagerness but with a happy sigh, she freed his long, hard shaft, marveling at the sight of it, the feel of it in her hands.

"Love," he groaned as she took her sweet time stroking him, learning the feel of his member and figuring out what he liked.

He put his hands over hers. "When we get home, love, I'm going to bury this inside of you."

"I don't want to wait," she whispered. And then she leaned forward, licking the tip first, and heartened by his growl of satisfaction.

She smiled against the ridge. "I want to please you, my lord."

"Oh, love, you always do."

"Teach me," she pleaded, looking up at him with wide eyes as she slid the tip of his member between her lips, swirling her tongue the way he'd done to her when he'd licked her sex.

His head fell back with a groan. When he shoved his hands roughly into her coif, she thought he might tug her away, but instead, he guided her, so her mouth slid down his shaft. He moved her slowly, giving her time to adjust.

She could feel his thighs shaking beneath her hands from the restraint he was using.

She didn't want restraint. She wanted to drive him to distraction. She wanted to be used by him, to be taken roughly, the way she ached for it.

"Christ, pet," he whispered. "Your mouth feels so good."

She moaned around his girth because he felt good, too. He tasted like heaven as his familiar scent filled her nose. She sucked gently, stilling when his fingers tightened in her hair.

Was she doing it wrong?

But when his hips gave an instinctive jerk, thrusting deeper into her mouth, she felt a surge of triumph. She sucked harder, loving his answering growl.

She slid her lips up, letting his member glide out long enough to whisper a command of her own. "Show me, my lord. I want you to."

He groaned, his fingers so tight in her hair it tugged against her scalp. But he did as she asked, guiding her mouth over his length and then pumping into her, just like he did to her quim. She sucked and licked, opening her mouth as wide as it would go as he tugged her head down until the top of his shaft hit the back of her throat.

"That's it, love," he growled above her.

His words made her moan even as she fought a gag when he went too deep. But even then, she wanted more. Her sex was aching to be touched, her breasts so sensitive that every move made her tight nipples harder as they rubbed against her bodice.

He shoved a hand inside, plucking at her nipple as his other hand firmly guided her head up and down. He muttered coarse words that ought to have horrified her, demanding that she suck him, that she swallow his release, that she take him in as far as she could.

But his words and his rough handling made her so filled with desire she nearly came along with him when he exploded inside her mouth.

She nearly choked but was met with murmurs of "good girl" when she swallowed his semen and pulled back to face him.

"What did I do to deserve you?" he asked, his eyes half-closed and sleepy.

She grinned up at him, pushing aside the pain that threatened to swallow her whole at what was to come.

At the way she would eventually hurt him.

But better she hurt him once and be gone than spend a lifetime making him suffer.

CHAPTER SEVENTEEN

I T WAS SUCH a relief to have Philippa back in his bed again, Benedict let all his questions and concerns from earlier in the night fall by the wayside.

For the first time in days, she was back to being his Philippa. Teasing, brash, incorrigible...and intoxicating. Gone was the quiet, sad girl he'd be so worried about, and in her place was the vixen who'd first tempted him into her bed.

"What about this?" she asked as she stroked his cock. "Do you like it like that?"

He growled, burying his head between her breasts. "I like you touching me. However you want to touch me."

"Then put it in my mouth again," she said. "I love the way you taste."

She let out a whimper when his mouth closed over her breast, and he sucked hard on her tight, rosy bud. "Yes, more," she gasped, her hands burying in his hair and holding him close.

More. He'd give her more. He'd give her everything he had and more.

Her hips arched up. "I need you. I need all of you."

He grinned against her luscious tit. This woman would be the death of him. And he wouldn't have it any other way.

Her head fell back with a laugh when he rolled them, so she was on top of him. They were half-dressed, her gown falling off one shoulder and his shirt torn open. Her hair was half undone—she looked wild and wanton. Too good to be true.

He reached up and tore the gown even more, so her breasts spilled free, and he drank in the sight of her.

Christ, she was gorgeous.

And she was his.

The thought had him growling, propping up on his elbows for another taste of her tight nipples.

She cried out, her hips rocking against his torso looking for relief.

His mother was in this house somewhere, and servants were everywhere, but he couldn't bring himself to care about modesty. Their wedding day would be here soon enough, but it was much too far away to wait.

Her hands roamed over his chest. With anyone else, he might have flinched when she lingered on his scars, tracing the shape of them. Her gaze met his, and it was filled with a question.

"Touch me," he said. "Touch me however you like."

Because I am yours.

Because you are mine.

He swallowed the words for another time. Their wedding night, perhaps. By then maybe she'd be more confident with this arrangement. Hopefully, she'll have fully embraced that this thing between them was real.

That their future would be a good one, despite their wretched pasts.

She took him at his word, her hands ruthless in their exploration until they were both panting with need. He went to take over, but she grabbed his hands and gave him a wicked grin. "Let me."

He chuckled, holding his hands up in surrender and tucking them under his head as she bent down and kissed every inch of him that she'd just touched.

Her lips were a brand, hotter than the fire that had melted his skin. By the time she'd trailed those lips down to his straining member and freed him, he was shaking with the effort to hold still.

She gripped his shaft gently and peeked up at him as if for permission, even as she spread her legs wide and straddled him. "May I, my lord?"

He groaned. He'd never get tired of that teasing, mischievous look. Her playacting the part of a submissive little innocent. He knew exactly what she wanted in return, and he hardened his stare into a glare. "Take me inside of you, pet."

Her lips parted, and her eyes grew dazed as she scrambled to do his bidding.

"That's it," he said as she angled her hips over him, lining him up with her tight entrance. "Sit on it, slide it in…" He broke off with an oath as she did as she was told, taking him into her sweet, wet heat. "Good girl," he muttered.

Her inner muscles clamped around him at the praise.

"Now ride me, love," he ordered. "Ride me until you come."

"Yes," she whimpered, her hips already rolling back and forth, up and down as she found a rhythm that suited her. "Yes, my lord."

He gripped her hips to help her, but soon she was tossing her head back, her hair hanging down to his thighs. Her eyes were closed, and her lips parted. And despite the growing tension in his loins, he was struck by a tenderness so overwhelming it left him winded.

She was perfect. Wild and free and passionate and loving.

She was perfect.

And she was his.

Much later that night, after they'd both found relief multiple times over, he tucked her into his arms and held her tight.

In the morning, he told himself. In the morning he'd ask her about why she'd sought out Foley, why she'd looked so guilty when he'd come over to claim her.

But when the sunlight woke him, his arms were empty. And by his side…was a note.

>>>>«««

"WHAT DO YOU mean, she's gone?" Hayden's eyes were puffy, his hair disheveled. He looked far worse for the wear as he stumbled down the steps of his townhome.

His butler who'd fetched him hovered nearby looking wary about whether he was supposed to be hearing this.

He shouldn't. The fewer people who knew that she'd run away, the better.

But mostly Benedict couldn't bring himself to care. He'd deal with the rumors and the scandal and whatever aftermath was to come…

After he brought her home.

"She left," he said again. "She's with Foley, I know it."

"What…How…" Hayden scrubbed a hand over his face, and his expression hardened into grim lines. "Right. Doesn't matter." He turned to the butler. "Wake Martin. Have him ready the horses. Send a message to Lord Raffian—"

"Already done," Benedict said. "He should be on his way—"

A hard banging at the front door interrupted.

"That'll be him."

"I should have murdered that bastard when I'd had the chance." Raff stormed past the butler. "I came as soon as I could. Where do you think they've gone?"

Benedict's jaw was clenched so tight he thought it might break. The note had not specified, but knowing Foley's history and knowing her…

"Gretna Green," he bit out.

His friends stared at him in horror.

"Why would she do such a thing?" Hayden asked.

Raff glowered, his hands clenching into fists. "Does he have something over her?"

Benedict shook his head.

"Over you?" Hayden asked.

"No. She's gone willingly." To admit it nearly killed him. His friends didn't pester him with questions but, as they were even now rallying to help him find her, they deserved to understand.

"She's punishing herself," he said, his gaze going dark with rage. But that was better than the cold, merciless fear that had been clawing at his insides ever since he woke to an empty bed.

"Punishing herself?" Raff echoed in confusion.

"And saving you," Hayden said softly.

Hayden seemed to have grasped it, and his gaze was filled with pity.

For Benedict or for Philippa, he did not know.

"That's it exactly." Benedict ran a hand over his face, barely noticing the scars that used to shock him anew every time he felt them. But now they were a part of him, just as his tragedy and his past were a part of him.

Just as Philippa was a part of him.

"She thinks she can outrun her past," he said, dropping his hand to his side. "She thinks she doesn't deserve a good life. A happy life."

The life he offered.

"I have to stop her," he said. If his friends were as shocked as he was by the desperation in his voice, they didn't let on.

Everyone was moving into action. Horses were saddled, and a plan was enacted. They'd be heading toward Scotland quickly, as they must have known that he'd be in pursuit. His nostrils flared as he nudged his horse to go fast.

Philippa couldn't have one second believed that he would let her go without a fight.

Hell, even if he found her married, he wasn't about to let her go. He'd steal another man's wife if he had to. He'd take her abroad and out of the reach of Foley or the law.

Foley wouldn't fight for her once he had her money.

But Benedict…

He wouldn't stop fighting until she was his.

CHAPTER EIGHTEEN

I T WAS A mistake. Philippa had done her part. She'd sent the hired carriage back to London, and there was no turning back now.

She eyed the inn where she and Foley had planned to meet.

But this was a mistake.

Her insides felt like rotten meat. Her eyes were burning with the need to weep. The carriage ride here had been an act of torture—regret and grief piercing her skin anew with each jolt and jerk of the vehicle.

He'd follow.

Benedict could even now be riding in this direction. Which was why she'd planned to meet Foley at the inn. It would be faster for them both, and they'd be harder to track leaving the city.

But he had to know where they were going.

She wrapped her cloak tighter around herself as two rough-looking men with scruffy beards eyed her from the stables beside the inn.

She shouldn't have left a note, maybe that would have bought her time.

She could have made some excuse about going shopping and then ditched her maid. She could have made so many plans much smarter than this one.

Wicked, evil girl.

Philippa might be wicked, but she'd never been a fool. And this plan was foolish. Almost like she wanted him to follow her.

Like she was begging to be caught.

She swallowed hard. Foley would be waiting for her inside. There was no turning back now.

Her head fell back, and she looked up at the gray, cloud-covered sky. Were her parents watching? Were they shaking their heads in disgust at yet another disaster she'd created?

Probably.

But they weren't here anymore to call her out on her bad behavior. She had no one.

No. She had Benedict.

And he would call her a fool, yes, but he would not think her evil. She tilted her head back to face the sky just as the droplets began to fall.

Rain.

She shut her eyes as memories washed over her.

She'd been a fool that night, too. Had she really thought her parents would just let her go? Or had she wanted them to chase her? Had she wanted to make them show her that they cared, even if it was just to prove that they wouldn't let her go without a fight?

She sniffled and pulled her cloak tighter still. There was no turning back now. She'd do what she set out to do. It might be a foolish path, but it was better than the alternative.

She pushed the door open and was greeted by a waft of warm, stale air and a roomful of beady-eyed stares as the locals assessed her.

Meanwhile, she scanned the crowd for any sign of Foley.

He was there, on the far side of the inn, sitting by the fire with a tankard of ale in his hand. She just barely held back a weary sigh.

He'd ridden here on horseback and must not have slept after the masquerade if his appearance was anything to go by. He grinned at the sight of her, and the smile was sloppy.

The fool was in his cups?

They had a lengthy journey ahead of them, and they were meant to ride his horse until the next stop, where they'd ditch the horse and join the next carriage heading their direction.

"Come," he said, patting the seat beside him. "Get warm before we set out."

She wanted to argue, but then again, she was chilled through, and she couldn't exactly leave without him.

He pushed his ale toward her, but she pushed it back. He didn't seem to notice because he lifted his hand, signaling the barmaid for another.

"What are you doing?" she asked with a frown.

"Celebrating." His eyes gleamed with triumph. "My father said I couldn't do it, you know."

"Oh, yes?" She did not even try to feign interest. The man might have some cleverness about him and was excellent at manipulation, but when she looked at him now, all she saw was weakness.

A weak chin, a sniveling voice going on about his father's approval...or lack thereof.

She tried to keep the look of disgust from her face, though she couldn't say who she was more disgusted by, herself or him.

Either way, they were co-conspirators now, she supposed. Two wicked knaves together forever. She eyed the ale with narrowed eyes. Perhaps she should numb her senses for what was to come.

"He thinks I'm useless," Foley continued, his lips curled in a sneer.

It took her a moment to realize he was still talking about his father. "I'm sorry."

And despite the fact that he was a cad and quite possibly a useless one at that...she did feel a pang of pity at the wretched emotions in his eyes.

"Doesn't matter," he said, waving his mug and sloshing ale

over the sides. "Because I'll prove him wrong, won't I?" He grinned at her. "We'll prove them all wrong, you and I."

Her chest contracted at being dragged into this. She wasn't looking to prove anything to anyone.

Aren't you?

She shook off the thought but her mind persisted.

Foley was trying to prove his father wrong. And she...

She was proving her father right. Was there a difference, really? They were both letting their fathers drive their actions.

Philippa reached for the mug and took a swallow as if that could rid her of the bitter taste.

"He thinks I don't have what it takes," Foley continued. "Thinks I have no chance of success just because I wasn't born first. The old fool." He leaned in toward her. "I can't wait to see the look on his face when he realizes I married an heiress."

She flinched as his hot, stale breath hit her in the face.

"Can't wait to see the look on all their faces," he continued in a mutter. "The Duke of Raffian and his wife? Oh, they won't be able to snub me now, will they?"

She squirmed in her seat at the mention of Evangeline. If there'd been any chance she might have made a friend in England, she was ruining that now.

"And your earl." His head fell back with a laugh. "Oh, I wish I could see that pompous arse's face when he realizes that I stole his betrothed."

"You did not steal anything," she bit out, her cheeks flushed as her heart twisted painfully. She'd been trying her best not to imagine Benedict's expression when he saw her gone...when he read her note of farewell...

She shouldn't have left it. She should have just left and bought herself more time.

The thought had her nudging Foley's arm. "They won't be far behind us, you know. The longer you sit here celebrating, the more likely we are to fail."

He nodded even as he waved her off. "We'll be fine. Plenty of time."

She stared at him for a long while trying to make sense of him. It seemed he wanted this more than anything. He'd been willing to blackmail a duke to get a fortune, for heaven's sake. But here he was, the time to act at hand...

And he was ruining his own chances. He was sabotaging his own plan. Almost like he wanted to be caught.

Aren't you doing the same?

She stared at him in horror. It wasn't as though she were making any move to push or prod him toward the door. And even as she'd written that farewell note, she'd understood the response it would evoke.

He would come for her.

Was she just like Foley? A self-destructive wastrel, just waiting to be caught and punished?

Despite the hot fire, a cold sweat broke out and trickled down her neck. What if he didn't come for her? Would she really go through with this? Give her family's fortune to a fool who didn't deserve it to be squandered just to appease her guilt?

Give her body to a man who did not care about her?

Hurt the one man who'd ever treated her with kindness and affection?

The one man who might possibly understand her and forgive her and help her become the kind of person she'd always wanted to be?

Not wicked. Not evil.

That wasn't her.

It didn't have to be her.

But what she was doing now...this was cruel. She dropped her head into her hands.

Oh, what was she doing? She could be snuggled up in bed with Benedict right now. She could be planning her wedding to the man that she...

Her head came up with a jerk.

Foley was still rambling beside her, but she could barely hear a word over the hectic pounding of her heart.

He was the man she loved.

And she was leaving him.

"He thinks I'm reckless." Foley leaned in toward her, and she backed away in disgust. "I'm not reckless. I'm just quick to seize opportunities. There's a difference, you know."

She stared at him with a frown.

She did know. Her parents had called her evil and wicked, but she wasn't. She knew that. Benedict had helped her to see it without even trying.

For the first time since she'd told Benedict that tragic tale the other night, she let herself go back to that night. The rain now pounding outside the inn's windows only helped her to feel as if time was turning backward. Not to the moment of her parents' crash, but earlier. Just before. The way she'd been feeling when she'd fled her home.

She'd been desperate. Heartbroken. Misunderstood by her parents, who seemed intent on thinking the worst of her. And she'd acted recklessly, yes.

Reckless—but not cruel.

There was a difference. Reckless was not evil.

Her heart was pounding so fiercely now, it drowned out the furious rainstorm, but she focused on the blurred scene outside the window as if she could see Benedict coming.

God, she'd done it again.

He'd chase after her despite the horrid weather. But she didn't want him to get hurt any more than she'd wished ill upon her parents.

She was up and out of her seat before she fully knew what she was doing.

"Not ready yet," Foley slurred beside her.

Philippa blinked down at him. For a moment, she'd almost forgotten him. Pity swelled inside of her as she watched him drown his self-hatred in ale. This would be her if she continued down this path of self-destruction.

She knew it as surely as she knew that a life with Benedict could be her salvation. A way forward rather than trying to punish herself by proving her father right.

Foley seemed to realize she was still standing beside him, and he turned his face upward to glare at her, his eyes narrowed in suspicion. "Told you, I'm not ready yet."

No. He wouldn't be. She had to wonder: was Foley just as intent on being caught? Maybe not consciously, but his actions now seemed to point toward it. He was a self-fulfilling prophecy, carrying out his father's ideas about who he was and what he was worth.

But it was Foley who chose to run off with her today, not his father.

It was Foley who'd chosen to lose himself in drink rather than ensure a swift journey.

Foley was making his choices even now by choosing not to act. It wasn't his father making him reckless; it was him who was acting reckless to prove his father right.

Her breathing was growing shallow. Why was it so much easier to see this in someone else? Maybe because she was too close to her own tragedies, her parents' voices too firmly fixed in her memories.

But she did not need to let them rule her.

She did not need to make them right.

She took a step away from Foley, her heart racing now as she knew what she must do.

The moment she made the decision, her body clamored for it to be done now. Impatience like she'd never known clawed at her. She had to get to Benedict.

She had to make this right.

She opened her mouth to tell Foley she'd been wrong. That this was a mistake. But he snarled up at her, the drunken haze gone from his eyes as he captured her wrist. "Where do you think you're going without me?"

"Changed my mind about the drink," she said with a smile

meant to appease. "You were right. We can't go anywhere until this rain eases up anyway. Might as well enjoy ourselves, right?"

The suspicion was still there, but he eased his grip. "See what's holding her up with my drink, too, eh?"

"Of course." Philippa hurried over to the barmaid and made sure that Foley's drink would come shortly. And that they wouldn't stop coming until he was blind drunk.

CHAPTER NINETEEN

B ENEDICT COULD HARDLY see more than a foot in front of his face, the rain was so blinding.

"Which way?" Hayden shouted.

Raff was leading his steed to a copse of trees off the road to get some shelter from the piercing, cold rain.

Hayden and Benedict followed.

"We'll need to wait it out," Raff said. "Just until it lightens."

Benedict nodded, his jaw too tightly clenched to speak. This fear was intolerable, so much worse than the anger.

Anger he could handle. Even the past year's shame and regret he could manage to keep in check. But fearing for Philippa was threatening to tear him apart.

His sanity was on the brink, and only the knowledge that she needed him had him holding himself together.

"We'll find her, Benedict." Hayden was uncharacteristically solemn beside him.

Benedict nodded. It was all he could do.

"We'll find *them*," Raff repeated, his features set in a glower as he tightened his grip on his reins. "And when we do, I'll do what I should have done the moment Foley entered our lives. I'll kill the bloody knave."

Benedict wished he could feel anger toward Foley. He would...once Philippa was safe in his arms.

He'd relish murderous rage right about now. Anything other than this terrifying sensation that something more precious than his own life was at stake, and there was nothing he could do about it.

Philippa meant more to him than anything. She was his heart now; she'd taken up residence inside his chest, and there she would stay...whether or not she returned.

Why hadn't he told her that when he'd had the chance?

"We'll find her, Benedict," Raff repeated Hayden's vow, and Benedict gave another short nod. He would find her. Even if he had to travel to the ends of the earth or steal her back using nefarious means or—

He blinked as a dark form took shape in the distance. Peering through the rain, he wondered if his mind was playing tricks on him.

Who would be riding like hell was nipping at their heels in weather like this? It was reckless and—

His heart leapt into a gallop as hope ran roughshod over sense.

"Benedict, where are you going?" Hayden shouted after him.

He didn't pause to answer, nudging his horse into a trot to head out from under the protection of the leaves for a better view. With the rain pouring down in sheets and trickling into his eyes, it was impossible to see much more than a brown mare, a dark, huddled figure and...

Red hair.

Tendrils clung to her cheek, but he caught the vivid red of her hair as it peeked out from beneath her hood. He rode directly into her path. "Philippa!"

Her head came up, and with wide eyes, she pulled on the reins, bringing the horse up on its hind legs.

For a second his heart faltered. He was certain she'd lose her grip and her balance between the rearing horse and the unforgiving rain. But she clung to its neck, and he could hear her murmuring to the mare as she slid down.

He was already there waiting for her, collecting her into his arms and holding her to his chest before her feet could even touch the ground.

Her arms wrapped around his neck, and she buried her face in his neck with a sob. "I'm sorry," she wept next to his ear. "I'm so sorry."

For a long moment, he could say nothing. All he could do was hold her tight, reassuring himself that she was here. That she was safe and whole and in his arms.

Exactly where she belonged.

"I'm so sorry," she kept repeating, her words interrupted by hiccupping sobs as she clung to him. He shifted her in his arms, so she was cradled against his chest.

"Is she all right?" Raff asked. He and Hayden had left their horses to rush over.

"Are you hurt, love?" he asked.

She shook her head.

"She will be," he answered Raff. "I have to get her home."

"Where's Foley?" Raff was looking behind her in confusion.

For good reason. Now that Benedict's heart was functioning and the tight knot of fear was dissolving, his mind was filled with questions.

Where was Foley? And what had she been doing riding in this weather by herself...back toward London?

Had something happened? He squeezed her even tighter, his gaze raking over her. Aside from the tears, she seemed to be uninjured. Hope filled him suddenly. Had she been coming back to him?

She lifted her head and finally stopped saying she was sorry to speak to Raff directly. "I left Foley at the inn about two miles down the road. He'll still be there."

"How do you know?" Raff asked.

She sniffled loudly. "Because I got him drunk and took his horse."

For a moment all three men stared at her. But then Hayden

and Raff looked at Benedict, and he could see them battling amusement. "We'll go deal with Foley," Hayden said. "You get your lady home safe."

He nodded his thanks. For all the anger that normally coursed through his veins, he couldn't even muster up a grudge against Foley at the moment.

All that mattered was here in his arms, and Foley could be left to rot for all he cared.

"Easy, love," he said when she started weeping all over again, burying her face in his neck. "I've got you."

HOURS LATER, HIS love was dry and warm, wrapped in blankets before a roaring fire.

"I am sorry, Benedict," she said. Her eyes were puffy, her nose red, but she'd ceased weeping, and for that, he was infinitely grateful.

He never felt more helpless than when watching Philippa cry.

He tugged her closer against his side, using his body to keep her warm. "So, you've said." With a smirk, he added, "Many times."

"Will you forgive me?" Her eyes were wide and still wet from her earlier tears.

He sighed, reaching out a hand to tilt her chin up, so she was forced to meet his gaze directly. "Love, I think the real question is…will you forgive yourself?"

She was quiet, her lips pressing together as she swallowed hard. Finally, she nodded. "You're right. I know you're right. I didn't leave because I didn't want you—"

"I know," he said.

"I left because I felt I didn't deserve what you were offering."

"I know that, too." He moved his hand, so he was cupping her cheek. Never had anyone or anything been so precious to him as this woman.

It was terrifying and perfect. To have all his priorities, his goals and dreams and vision of the future so totally shifted because of one woman...

Well, it was life-changing. She gave him a future where before he'd only had duty and obligation. If only he could give her the same. He wanted to, but it was becoming clear that it wasn't just about what he wanted for her.

She had to want it to.

"And now?" he asked. "What changed, love? Why did you come back?"

Her lips trembled, and she pressed her cheek into his hand like she could soak up his warmth. "I don't know if I'll ever fully forgive myself for my reckless actions," she said slowly. "And truthfully, I don't know if I'll ever feel like I deserve you."

His heart clenched painfully as her voice hitched.

"But listening to Foley talk, seeing how he wasn't acting but rather reacting to his father's opinions of him..." She shook her head. "I suppose I saw it then. Just how much I'd been basing my decisions and my actions on others' opinions. I don't believe that I am so very wicked."

His chest tightened again at the conflict in her eyes as she tried to sort through her feelings and her beliefs.

"I know that I never set out to hurt anyone," she said slowly. "I know I have my faults, but I also know..." Her gaze met his, and she reached a hand up to cover his. "I also know I have a lot of love to give."

He slid his hand around to the back of her head and tugged her close for a hard kiss. He couldn't speak if he tried, but he could show her what that meant to him.

"I'm responsible for my own actions from here on out," she said, her voice firm. "I'll not let my past dictate my future."

Pride made his heart swell as he watched his little spitfire become stronger right in front of his eyes.

"I choose who I want to be," she said.

A smile tugged at his lips. "And who is that?"

Her eyes welled with tears, but so much of the pain that clouded them lifted as she spoke. "Your wife."

"Love," he growled, tugging her into his arms.

"The mother of your children," she continued.

He kissed her hard, his lips claiming hers, and his tongue tasting her sweet warmth. "I love you," he rasped when he finally pulled back. "I should have told you before. I should have said it the moment I'd realized—"

"I love you, too." She interrupted him with the breathy whisper, her voice thick with emotions as she leaned into his embrace and buried her face in his neck. "I love you so much, Benedict. I knew that even before I left, I just…I'm so sorry it took nearly losing you for me to realize that hurting us both wouldn't make up for my past."

He kissed her temple, stroked her back. "I would have tracked you down, you know. You wouldn't have been able to run from me forever."

He felt her smile against his cheek. "I know."

His arms tightened around her, and they held each other tight, reassuring themselves that no one was going anywhere.

"It was so foolish to try and run from my past when what I should have been doing was embracing my future." She turned to rest her forehead against his. "And you are my future."

They were interrupted by a sharp knock on the door before his mother poked her head in. She wore a frown as she studied them both. "Where did you two get off to in this wretched weather?"

He and Philippa exchanged a wary look. The fewer people who knew about her near desertion the better. He had no doubt Raff and Hayden would ensure Foley's silence, but he didn't relish lying to his mother.

Luckily, she seemed to realize no answer was forthcoming. Her gaze met Philippa's. "Doesn't matter. What matters now is that you are here. With us." Her eyes darted over to meet

Benedict's. "With family."

Philippa rested a hand on his arm and squeezed as Benedict gave his mother a short nod of understanding.

It wasn't much of an olive branch, but they were heading in the right direction. All of them. It might not be easy, but together they would be a family, and they'd teach each other how to forgive and how to move forward.

His mother left them again, and for a long while, they sat together in silence, each lost in memories and thoughts about the past and the future.

"I am sorry, you know. I promise you, I won't do anything to take your love for granted ever again."

"You'd better not," he said gruffly, his lips pressed against her hair. "You're mine now, you know. You're mine, and I'm never letting you go."

He felt her smile against his lips as she kissed him sweetly. "I am yours, my lord." The hint of mischief in her voice had his cock stirring like a dog begging for a bone. He growled, loving her giggle as she shifted in his arms, pressing her soft curves into his hard chest.

"It was awfully naughty of me to run off, though, don't you think?" she asked, her voice so breathless he couldn't help but nip at her neck.

"Naughty? It was outright disobedient, love."

Her breathing grew shallow and her hands insistent as he tugged her onto his lap. His hard length dug into her bottom.

"Oh dear," she whispered. "It sounds like I'm in trouble."

He half laughed and half growled as he shifted her in his arms, his saucy little minx. "Oh, my love. It's time we teach you a lesson then…"

"Yes, please," she sighed, her thighs already parting to straddle him. "Show me how I can make it up to you."

He tugged up her skirts and nipped at her lower lip. "I'll do better than that, pet. I'll show you just how much I love you. Exactly how you are. Good, bad, naughty, or wicked. I love you.

All of you."

Her eyes were wet with tears as she leaned back to look at him. "I love you, too, Benedict. And right here with you…I have the family I've always wanted." She swallowed thickly as she gave him a watery smile. "*You* are the family I've always deserved."

EPILOGUE

One month later...

P HILIPPA HAD THOUGHT that perhaps the revelry might die down once the wedding breakfast was complete.

She'd been wrong.

Laughter bubbled up inside her at the sight of a drunken Marquess of Hayden tugging a reluctant Lady Raffian onto the dance floor in the midst of their country manor's drawing room.

There were no musicians at this morning's fete, nor even a lady playing upon the pianoforte. But that did not stop the incorrigible Lord Hayden from whirling a laughing Evangeline about the room as her husband looked on with tolerant exasperation. "You do know that is *my* wife, yes?"

"Of course," Hayden said cheerfully.

Lord Raffian sighed, but there was laughter in his eyes as he watched his wife giggle along with his friend. "He's insufferable," Raff said to Philippa, who stood beside him.

"But entertaining," she added with a grin.

"I'm glad you think so. Some ladies might fear a rogue like Hayden would ruin their perfect day."

Philippa laughed softly as she cast a glance over toward her new husband, who was conversing with the Earl of Fallenmore and his wife. But even while speaking to others, Benedict's dark gaze was fixed on her from across the room, along with a small, affectionate smile that made her heart do a flip in her chest. "Nothing could ruin this day, my lord," she murmured.

Raff's chuckle was knowing. "I would imagine not. Benedict has been driving us to distraction as he waited for this day to finally come about."

"It was hardly a lengthy engagement," she said.

Though it *had* felt like an age. While she'd been enjoying this day thoroughly, she was more than a little eager to be alone with her new husband.

But if he were just as frustrated with pent-up desire, then it was his own fault. The day after she returned from her ill-fated trip with Mr. Foley, Benedict had decided that they ought to do things properly for once.

The exact words he'd used were, *we ought to take things slowly.* She teased him that staying out of her bed was the worst sort of punishment of all, but he'd grown frighteningly serious as he explained his reasoning.

You deserve to be courted, he'd said. *You deserve to be wooed and flirted with and treated the way a gently bred young lady ought.*

She'd gone to argue. They were well past flirtation and courtship, after all. But she'd seen what it meant to him, and she'd known very well that he was doing this for her. That he wanted this marriage to begin as they meant for it to continue.

With mutual respect and trust...and without the guilt and regrets that had driven them together in the first place.

Despite the fact that she ached to be in his arms again, Philippa could admit that perhaps he'd been right to insist upon this time together spent as friends and as a new couple.

But she was still counting the seconds until they were finally alone as man and wife.

"Ah, there you are." Benedict's mother—her new mother-in-law, Philippa realized with a start—stood beside her and sighed at Hayden's antics. "I suppose it would have been too much to hope that all of Benedict's friends had outgrown their careless ways."

Philippa pressed her lips together to stifle a smile because even the dour and formidable dowager countess seemed to be holding back a laugh as they watched Hayden and Evangeline dance.

"Thank you for everything you've done, my lady," Philippa said. "You made today a truly special occasion and—"

"Mother," she interrupted abruptly.

Philippa blinked. "Pardon?"

The dowager sniffed. "I'd like it if you call me Mother. If...if you wish it."

Philippa's eyes widened with surprise. Benedict's mother had been making more of an effort to spend time with them these past few weeks, joining them on strolls through the park and even occasionally playing cards with them in the evening.

But this still seemed out of character for the standoffish woman.

The dowager countess turned to her with a wry twist of her lips. "You don't have to look so shocked, dear. I'd have embraced you as part of our family solely because Benedict chose you as his wife. But aside from that, I am quite fond of you."

Philippa's lips parted. Was she? She'd known the other woman tolerated her, but she wouldn't have guessed she felt affection for Philippa.

The older woman's face softened. "You remind me so much of your mother when she was young."

Philippa braced for it, but a flicker of pain still lanced through her. "So you've said."

Many times.

The dowager countess tsked. "Not just in looks, you know. Your mother shared your spirit."

Philippa blinked in surprise. "Did she?"

"Oh, yes." The dowager countess looked so much younger when her eyes sparkled with laughter. "She was always getting into trouble when we were young."

Philippa gaped at the other woman. "She did?"

The dowager countess's laugh was a cackle as her face softened with memories. "Oh, the stories I could tell you. She drove your grandmother mad with her wicked ways."

Philippa stared some more, her words coming out on a breath as she fumbled for words. "Did she?"

"And your father, too, from what I understand."

Philippa gasped. "No."

"Oh yes. Before they settled down to be near his family in Italy, they were wild and free-spirited. Truthfully, I was surprised that they'd settled at all."

Philippa's mind raced with questions, and for the first time in more than a year, talk of her parents made her want to laugh instead of cry. "I would love to hear more about them," she said. "About what they were like…"

The dowager smiled and patted her arm. "Of course, dear."

"Mother," Benedict's deep voice behind her interrupted the moment. "Are you enjoying yourself?"

"I am," she said. And she sounded genuine. "But I see some guests whom I ought to speak with. If you'll excuse me…" She took her leave to speak with the older crowd, who were looking on with a mix of amusement and shock at Benedict's friends' behavior.

Benedict lowered his voice for her ears only. "And how does my *wife* fare?" His hand came to her lower back as he stood between her and Raff.

She tilted her head back to meet his gaze and was very nearly swept off her feet by the love she saw there.

"I'm having the most wonderful day," she said truthfully. "And you?"

His smile warmed her heart as he leaned in to speak closely to her ear. "I'll be better once everyone is gone, and you and I are alone."

She laughed. "Patience, my love."

He growled in response, but his smile never faltered as he pressed a kiss to her temple. "But I, too, am having a wonderful day." His smile widened. "The best day of my life."

"With many more to come," she said.

They shared a sweet smile that was broken by laughter from the small crowd around them.

"To think," Lady Fallenmore murmured beside her. "I always thought marquesses were meant to be so very proper."

Philippa laughed. Philippa had become fast friends with the Earl of Fallenmore's new wife. As a widow and the daughter of a businessman who ran London's most salacious scandal sheet, Lady Fallenmore was a fellow outcast in good society.

She and Evangeline had taken Philippa in as a friend, while Benedict's old school companions had been kind enough to pretend that day out in the rain had never happened.

In all, Philippa was aware she'd been very lucky indeed when she'd met Benedict. Not only did she find the love of her life, but she'd found a family, too.

An odd family, perhaps. But she wouldn't have it any other way.

"Here you are," Hayden said with a flourish as he handed a flushed and laughing Evangeline over to her husband. "I thank you for allowing me to borrow your wife."

"Allow?" Raff scoffed, his arm coming around his wife's waist. "As if I had a choice."

Evangeline smiled sweetly and planted a kiss on his cheek, which had his feigned anger fading into a grin.

"Perhaps it's time you stop stealing other men's wives and find a wife of your own, Hayden," Benedict said as he tugged Philippa close to his side.

"You are the last man standing," Lord Fallenmore pointed out.

Hayden scowled. "Three out of the four of us married. Isn't that good enough for you?"

Raff arched a brow. "The trouble is, Hayden, none of our wives can help you to sire an heir."

This was met with laughter from the ladies, and Hayden

sighed dramatically. "It's not like I haven't tried. I've danced with every pretty young lady in the *ton*. I've been to more soirees and theater outings and picnics and strolls and…" He trailed off with a shake of his head. "And for what?"

"You did promise to find a wife this season," Benedict pointed out, laughter in his eyes at his friend's expense."

"And the season is almost over," Raff warned.

Philippa took pity on her new friend. "You cannot force him to marry if he hasn't found a lady who appeals to him. Like he said, he's met them all."

"Not *all*," Lord Fallenmore said, his gaze meeting his wife's in a silent exchange.

With her connections to the scandal sheet and her acquaintance with those spies who provided all the best gossip, Lady Fallenmore tended to know everything going on in society—for better or worse.

She was a keeper of secrets, she liked to say…which made her a truly excellent friend, indeed.

"Tell us," Philippa demanded.

"Do you have someone in mind for our dear Hayden?" Evangeline added.

Hayden was grimacing as if readying for a blow.

"It's a rather sordid tale…" Lady Fallenmore started hesitantly.

"My favorite kind," Hayden shot back.

The Earl of Fallenmore stepped in with a warning look. "She's a young lady in need of saving, not necessarily by marriage."

"A damsel in distress, eh? I like the sound of it even more now," Hayden said. He adopted a roguish grin. "One last grand adventure before I resign myself to a tedious marriage."

Benedict's tone was dry. "You are aware that you are currently in attendance at a wedding, are you not?"

"Don't try and change his mind on marriage, Benedict," Raff laughed. "There are some things a man must learn for himself."

Hayden ignored that, turning to Lady Fallenmore instead. "Now, tell me about this lady who needs saving, and I shall rush to her rescue."

The Earl of Fallenmore winced. "Right now? You're well in your cups old chap."

Hayden waved him off as he took Lady Fallenmore to the side to question her on this lady in need of his assistance.

Philippa glanced up at Benedict. "Is he in earnest?"

"About saving the young lady in question?" He grinned. "Most definitely. For all his faults, Hayden has never been able to resist a damsel in distress."

She started to laugh. "Oh dear."

"Precisely," Benedict said as he tugged her closer in his arms. "Fallenmore knows this well, and I suspect that's why he brought it up."

Philippa turned to watch Benedict's friends closely. "You are truly devious, aren't you?"

His laugh was a low rumble as he kissed the top of her head. "Would you want us any other way?"

She grinned up at him. "Definitely not."

About the Author

Bella Moxie is the author of the steamy regency romance series, *Dukes Gone Dirty*, as well as the offshoot novella series, *Rogues Gone Dirty*. Her books are spicy, but filled with sweet, satisfying, over-the-top love that not even the most alpha hero can resist.

Grab a free, steamy regency romance novella when you join Bella's newsletter at:
eepurl.com/gW_QWL

Lightning Source UK Ltd.
Milton Keynes UK
UKHW020123090622
404155UK00012B/125